"WHAT MAKES YOU THINK I WANT SOMETHING?"

Drew asked.

"Because I know you. I know how your mind works." Andra held her glass up automatically to make it easier for him to refill it. "I've watched you play poker too many times not to recognize a bluff when I see one."

Drew cursed himself silently. He'd let his feelings for her almost wreck his game plan. If he wasn't careful she'd read him like a marked deck. She was the only person he'd ever known who could. He'd never let anyone else get that close.

"Drew, don't bluff me. This isn't a poker game, it's life . . . my life." Andra's voice was unsteady, her eyes deeply troubled. "The one thing you never did was play games with *me*."

Drew raised his eyes to hers. "But you're on the other side of the table now."

Dear Reader:

SILHOUETTE DESIRE is an exciting new line of contemporary romances from Silhouette Books. During the past year, many Silhouette readers have written in telling us what other types of stories they'd like to read from Silhouette, and we've kept these comments and suggestions in mind in developing SILHOUETTE DESIRE.

DESIREs feature all of the elements you like to see in a romance, plus a more sensual, provocative story. So if you want to experience all the excitement, passion and joy of falling in love, then SILHOUETTE DESIRE is for you.

For more details write to:

Jane Nicholls
Silhouette Books
PO Box 236
Thornton Road
Croydon
Surrey CR9 3RU

GINA CAIMI
Hearts are Wild

Silhouette Desire

Originally Published by Silhouette Books
division of
Harlequin Enterprises Ltd.

First published in Great Britain 1985
by Silhouette Books, 15–16 Brook's Mews, London W1A 1DR

© Gina Caimi 1985

Silhouette, Silhouette Desire and Colophon are Trade Marks of Harlequin Enterprises B.V.

ISBN 0 373 05218 9

225–1185

Printed and bound in Great Britain by
Cox & Wyman Ltd, Reading

GINA CAIMI

started making up her own fairy tales when she was six years old. It was the only way she could get through arithmetic class. She sculpts as a hobby, adores the opera, ballet, and old movies, but writing remains her major passion. And she still hates arithmetic.

Other Silhouette Books by Gina Caimi

Silhouette Desire

Passionate Awakening
A Wilder Enchantment

For further information about
Silhouette Books please write to:

Jane Nicholls
Silhouette Books
PO Box 236
Thornton Road
Croydon
Surrey CR9 3RU

1

~~000000000~~

Damned if he still wasn't the most devastatingly attractive man she'd ever met, Andra thought resentfully. The impact that seeing Drew again had on her senses took her totally by surprise, held her frozen in front of the swinging saloon doors that separated the poker pit from the rest of the casino.

With the trained eye of a photographer, she scanned the polished mahogany and brass fixtures, the fake Tiffany lamps, and the sawdust-covered floor of the lavishly recreated Wild West saloon. In Las Vegas, where nothing was left to chance—especially games of chance—the decor was a deliberate attempt to encourage the clientele to forget their workaday world and indulge their fantasies . . . while parting with their money as painlessly as possible.

The good ol' frontier days—when men were men

who played a rough, tough game of poker and women were saloon girls, there only to service the men's drinking and sexual needs—were just such a fantasy. And a pretty popular one at that, Andra thought, judging from the number of people who were playing or watching the games. Through the thick layers of smoke that colored the air like smog and halfway across the crowd-filled saloon, she'd spotted Drew instantly.

She told herself it was because of the sheer size of the man—even sitting down he managed to tower over everyone else at the table. Or it could have been the incongruous elegance of the evening clothes that he always wore when he worked. They gave him the dark, rakish look of a riverboat gambler from the turn of the century. Andra knew how deliberately Drew Ramsey had created that image, how perfectly he fit into this fantasy world. It saddened her for a moment. But she couldn't take her eyes off him.

The custom-made dinner jacket that molded his powerful shoulders and chest was as black as the ace of spades. It was just a shade darker than his gleaming hair, which he wore longer than was fashionable. It curled over the edge of the collar of his white silk, pleated-front shirt. His hair was so thick it looked wiry, but it was surprisingly soft to the touch, Andra knew. She was disturbed to find that she hadn't forgotten the way his bushy moustache tickled when he kissed her either. Especially when he trailed kisses down her . . .

Deliberately suppressing the memories and feelings that the sight of Drew was churning up inside her, Andra forced herself to concentrate instead on how unusually pale he was, even for a man who'd chosen

8

to live by night. He seemed thinner than she remembered also. The strong, dramatic lines of his face had a sharper edge to them, giving his high cheekbones and the jagged bump where his nose had been broken a more dangerous cast than before. But the soft, full curve of his lips still gave him away, hinting at the surprising tenderness and sensuality that he was capable of.

Andra couldn't see Drew's eyes, not even after she'd made her way to the brass railing that circled the playing area. They were hidden by his thick, black lashes, intent on watching the stubby hands of the man who was dealing the fourth card in a game of seven-card stud. Yet she could feel the intensity behind Drew's hooded gaze as he tried to calculate the odds from the face-up cards on the green baize-covered table, and "place" the hole cards of his four opponents.

Drew did everything with that fierce intensity, Andra recalled with an odd twinge of regret. That was what had first drawn her to him. She was sure that was what was drawing the crowd to him now. Games were in progress at all of the dozen or so poker setups, but most of the "railbirds"—the losers, the kibitzers, the merely curious enjoying a vicarious gamble—were crowding around the rail nearest his table. Andra found herself being pushed right up against the brass railing as they jostled for position. With that sixth sense peculiar to gamblers, they knew that the game was rapidly escalating into a fierce fight for survival.

It was not one of Drew's lucky nights. The cards were not running for him, and the man to his right was "on a rush," hitting hand after hand as if by magic.

Only one other man at the seven-sided table was losing more than Drew.

The man, in his early forties, had the strained face and desperate eyes of a compulsive gambler. He was drinking heavily and his game was erratic. His nicotine-stained fingers shook whenever he slid the chips from his rapidly diminishing pile into the pot. In spite of his heavy losses, he continued to play emotionally, against the odds, doubling up on his bets in a frantic attempt to recoup.

Sitting alongside him, a study in contrasts, was a white-haired executive type. Betting as cautiously as he drank, he played a smooth, evasive game. Rarely bumping, but occasionally bluffing, he wasn't an easy opponent to second-guess, yet he was barely breaking even.

To his left, complete with Stetson and lizard-skin boots, sat a lanky cowboy who, Andra was willing to bet, had never seen a cow in his life. Well, maybe a mechanical bull or two, she silently amended. With his manicured hands and smooth, unlined face, she had him pegged as an urban cowboy. He seemed to have an instinctive feel for the cards, knowing intuitively when to stay and when to throw in, and he was holding his own.

The big winner of the game sat at Drew's right, an unlit cigar clamped between his thick lips. He looked and acted like the king of the mountain. Appropriately, the stacks of chips massed in front of him were reminiscent of a mountain fortress. There were three high towers of black one-hundred-dollar chips, a couple of towers of gray five hundreds, and a smaller bastion of green twenty-fives. A big bull of a man in his mid-thirties, he wore a typically garish Las Vegas sport shirt that openly proclaimed him a tourist. Loud and a bit vulgar, with the overly friendly manner of a traveling salesman, he kept up a relentlessly joking patter while he dealt the final card face down.

The clumsy way that he handled the cards and his unprofessional manner gave Andra the impression that he was the least experienced gambler of the lot. His heavy betting and the aggressive way he kept trying to raise everyone out of his seat qualified him as a high roller.

Andra found herself holding her breath when, completing the final round of betting, he flipped over his hole cards. The backed-up kings he revealed beat out the remaining hands, including Drew's three queens. A somewhat amazed grin split the salesman's ruddy, thick-featured face. He seemed genuinely surprised by his own lucky streak.

Andra was just as surprised by the sudden painful constriction in her chest as she watched the man raking in the pot of over twenty thousand dollars. Reminding herself that Drew's welfare was no longer her concern didn't help.

The curvaceous cocktail waitress who'd been waiting just inside the opening in the brass rail for the hand to be played out made her way to the table with another round of drinks. In keeping with the Wild West motif, she wore an abbreviated dance-hall-girl costume. The emerald green fabric matched the color of her eyes and emphasized her auburn hair, as well as her more obvious charms. Black net opera hose and four-inch show-girl heels added allure to her long, shapely legs. A lace garter circled one perfectly proportioned thigh.

Positioning herself between Drew and the salesman, she bent over to serve the drinks. "Here you go," she said, smiling invitingly at Drew and serving him first.

Inviting smiles in Vegas, Andra recalled, were reserved solely for big winners. She couldn't help feeling a tiny twinge of jealousy.

"Are you sure this is all you want?" the waitress added. Because of her seductive drawl, Andra wondered whether the voluptuous redhead was really referring to the Perrier water she'd just served Drew. Although the drinks were on the house, mineral water was the only thing Drew touched when he worked.

If the cocktail waitress was offering a more personal kind of service, Drew didn't seem, or chose not, to notice. "This is fine," he replied politely while he continued gathering up the loose cards with sure hands. "Tell you what, though—we could use a fresh deck."

The salesman paused in the middle of stacking his newly won chips, adding another tower to his fortress. "What's with a new deck of cards at this stage of the game?"

Holding the pack in one hand, Drew ran his long, supple fingers lightly over the top edges of the cards, riffling them. "These are a bit worn around the edges," he explained evenly to the cocktail waitress, as though she were the one who'd made the complaint. He waited for her to finish collecting the empties.

"But we've only got a few more hands to play," the

big winner grumbled impatiently around his cigar. "And we're wasting time here."

"We'll play them." Drew tossed the deck of cards onto the girl's cork-lined tray with a cool smile. She hesitated for a moment, obviously aware that she was caught in the middle but not sure what to do about it. Then, noticing the no-nonsense glint in Drew's eyes, she hurried off without further hesitation.

"Well, if that doesn't beat all," the salesman muttered, barely able to contain his outrage.

Reaching coolly into the inside pocket of his jacket, Drew removed a gold cigarette case and matching lighter. Andra recognized them instantly. She had given them to him two years before, on his thirty-fifth birthday. Deliberately continuing to ignore the salesman, which only increased the latter's frustration, Drew snapped open the case and took out a cigarette.

"Stopping a hot game cold," the salesman protested bitterly. He knew the rules of the game—there was nothing he could do about it. That only made him angrier. He bit down on the burnt-out stub of his cigar. "I'm superstitious about changing cards when I'm running a lucky streak," he added, as if he felt that he needed to explain to the others why he was so upset.

Replacing the cigarette case and lighter, Drew exhaled a leisurely stream of smoke from the cigarette he'd just lit. "It's not the cards. It's the way you play them." He turned finally to face the salesman. Since Andra was standing behind the rail directly in back of the man, Drew caught sight of her for the first time.

He seemed to forget everything else for the moment, and undisguised pleasure flared in the depths of his eyes as they locked with hers. He still had the darkest eyes she'd ever seen, and the most compelling. At least they still affected *her* that way, Andra realized ruefully when she tried to break the connection and found that she couldn't.

She had the sudden unnerving sensation that nothing had changed between them. The time and distance that had separated them hadn't done their work after all. That was exactly what the triumphant little smile curving his lips seemed to imply.

Drew took a long, hungry drag on his cigarette while he read the bewilderment in Andra's expressive gray eyes with deep satisfaction. He scanned her newly styled ash-blonde hair, which was parted in the middle and cut to curve just under her chin, framing her face softly. With deliberation, he traced every delicate feature of her face, lingering on her soft, full lips as if he were reexperiencing the feel and taste of them. Nor did he bother to hide his reaction when his narrowing gaze moved down her body.

Andra's blue-striped shirtwaist dress was buttoned up to the collar and reached halfway down her calves, but it was precious little protection against Drew's memories. His darkening gaze glided over the high, round curve of her breasts and down her slim waist and the soft flare of her hips with that old possessiveness.

Where was his poker face now? she wondered angrily. The intensity with which he was staring at her was causing other people to look at her also. Even the salesman, who was busy muttering about how long "that bimbo" was taking to get the cards, turned to look at her.

Andra read the question mark in his beady eyes as

they skimmed over her slender body. With all the voluptuous "bimbos" wandering about, it was clear that he couldn't understand Drew's interest in her. He frowned suddenly, inexplicably, when he saw the patent leather handbag Andra hadn't realized that she was clutching for dear life.

The salesman turned back to Drew, but whatever he was about to complain about this time was forgotten as the cocktail waitress stopped by their table.

The stunning redhead offered Drew a fresh pack of cards and a fresh version of her inviting smile. He accepted the cards but passed on the smile again. In typical Las Vegas fashion, any personal disappointment she might have felt was forgotten instantly when Drew tossed a black hundred-dollar chip onto her tray. She gushed her thanks before hurrying over to the cashier's cage to cash it in.

With one flick of his thumb, Drew broke the seal and opened the packet. The cards slid easily into his expert hands, fitting into the supple contours of his palm as if that was what they'd been meant for.

Andra knew the feeling. She hated to admit it, but she knew that it was a sure bet she'd never forget it. In order to block out the disturbingly vivid memory of Drew's touch she forced herself to concentrate on the cards.

She watched his long, talented fingers fan the deck of cards out in an arc to make sure that it was complete. Flipping it over, face down, he mixed it flat on the table, Vegas fashion. After shuffling expertly, he offered the pack to the urban cowboy on his left for the cut. Drew called the game, seven-card stud, and began to deal.

The railbirds pressed forward with a low murmur of anticipation as the blue-backed cards glided surely, rhythmically out of his hands. In his deep, husky voice, he analyzed each card, calling the chances as they fell.

In spite of herself, Andra had to admire the way Drew played. His concentration was total. There were no wasted words or motions, no expression whatsoever on his ruggedly handsome face. And always, that controlled intensity. With his photographic memory, he knew at any point of the deal which cards had already fallen, how many were left in the pack, and how many would help him—just as he was able to calculate the exact odds on his making a hand and the precise percentages offered by every pot.

Playing a strong, aggressive game, Drew easily won the next two hands. His most aggressive calls and raises were directed at the salesman. It soon became obvious that Drew was playing against one adversary only. The others saw it too. One by one they dropped out, leaving the two of them to their duel.

Word of the game had spread through the casino in that almost mystical way a big winning streak or a blockbuster game was somehow telegraphed in Vegas. Thrill seekers as well as hard-core gamblers were abandoning the various gambling pits outside and drifting into the saloon. Excitement, edged with danger, crackled in the air like electricity. It flowed through the crowd of strangers straining against the railing, binding them together into a single hushed entity.

Andra had forgotten that poker could be a bloodless form of dueling. Wasn't that why the final move in the game was called the showdown? She licked her dry lips nervously as the urban cowboy dealt the fifth card.

Drew was showing a queen, a jack, and a nine. The salesman's up cards were stronger: a pair of kings and a seven.

Drew glanced quickly at the cards and knocked twice on the baize with a gray five-hundred-dollar chip. The salesman stared at him and then at the cards. Only his beady eyes moved. He hadn't expected Drew to check. He continued to consider Drew's possible straight and whether he was trying to run a bluff. Clamping down on his cigar stub, the salesman separated a couple of towers of chips from the fortress in front of him and pushed them toward the center. They collapsed with a tinkling sound onto the gray and black mound that was already lying there.

"Ten thousand," he announced confidently, almost defiantly. It was obvious that he meant to force Drew out of the game or, at the very least, to give him the worst possible odds for making his hand.

Drew leaned back in his chair and stared at the salesman, unblinking, for a full minute. While he considered the alternatives, he unconsciously danced the gray chip lightly over his knuckles. For endless minutes the two opponents faced one another.

Drew's hand stopped abruptly. Reaching over, he lifted a stack of gray five hundreds and, without seeming to count them, pushed them into the pot. He seemed utterly unconcerned, as though they were playing with pennies.

"You've got something down there, have you, boy?" Indicating Drew's hole cards, the salesman turned to the railbirds with a raucous laugh. He never lost an opportunity to play to them, Andra noted, his beady eyes lighting up when any of them applauded a big win. He muttered angrily when he lost, and a very real threat became evident behind his friendly facade.

Drew smiled coldly to show that he hadn't been taken in. He knew that his opponent's "coffee-housing" was verbal bluffing; a trick to get him to react, exposing his strength or weakness.

The dealer waited for the salesman to turn his attention back to the game before dealing the sixth card: an eight of clubs for the salesman and a four of diamonds for Drew.

Without a moment's hesitation, the salesman put his stubby hands behind his entire fortress of chips and pushed it to the center.

Andra gasped. It was lost in the communal gasp of the crowd. Everyone knew the bet was a gauntlet, to force Drew to fold or put his entire stack of chips in. It was a freeze-out—winner take all.

Casually, Drew put his hands behind his remaining chips and slid them into the pot.

The railbirds craned over, the murmuring stopped, and there was a long, aching silence. More money than most of them would earn in a year was riding on the turn of a card. Andra knew that Drew never thought about money when he played. It was just a stack of chips to him. But *she* knew that it was money—that had been one of their problems—and her stomach knotted up fifty thousand dollars' worth.

With Drew all in, there would be no more betting. Both antagonists turned over their hole cards for the showdown. Drew's were a jack and a ten. Since he was showing another jack, a queen, a nine, and a four, he now held a pair of jacks and a possible open-ended straight.

The salesman's hole cards were an ace and an eight. His face-up cards were a pair of kings, a seven, and another eight, giving him two pairs—the potentially winning hand.

The urban cowboy pushed his Stetson back on his head and cleared his throat. It sounded as dry and constricted as Andra's felt. In Vegas fashion, he burned—discarded—the top card and dealt the next card up to the salesman: a five of clubs. Although it didn't better his hand, the confident grin remained on the salesman's beefy face, but it seemed pasted on.

The dealer paused dramatically, like an actor who knows that the audience is hanging on his every gesture. Andra stopped breathing. Only a jack, king, or eight could save Drew. The cowboy burned the next card and dealt a jack of hearts. The crowd exploded. So did Andra. The salesman blinked once and did not move.

Andra had to grab onto the brass rail with both hands to stop herself from rushing over to Drew. Several spectators were already on their way to him. He was quickly surrounded by them and the wildly enthusiastic applause of the railbirds, yet he looked totally uninvolved.

Turning his head slowly, Drew glanced at Andra. An odd little smile twisted his mouth when he realized that she wasn't going to join the well-wishers. His attention was brought back to the table by one of the casino cashiers who'd just materialized at his side with a couple of racks for his chips.

"Shall I count it up for you, Mr. R.?" the cashier inquired with thoroughly trained politeness.

"Thanks, Pete." Getting to his feet, Drew stepped away from the poker table, allowing the cashier access to his winnings, as he finally acknowledged his well-wishers.

While congratulating him, Andra noticed, every one of them managed to touch Drew in some way—a tap on the arm, a small pat on the back or shoulder. There was something ritualistic about it, as if they believed that by touching him, his luck would rub off on them. There was a new, hopeful gleam in their eyes when they hurried off in their endless pursuit of Lady Luck.

The salesman, who'd been sitting there in stunned silence, suddenly charged out of his seat like a mortally wounded bull. He looked around in a confused way, as if in search of the torero who had done him in. His dazed eyes fixed on Andra's patent leather bag. She might have been waving a red cape from the way he hurled himself toward her. His voice was a bellow of enraged pain. "Hey, you!"

"Are you speaking . . . to me?" she mumbled incredulously.

"That's right, lady!" He cleared the opening in the railing but Drew was already on the move. With one swift, agile motion, he was in front of the salesman, shielding Andra with his powerful body.

"That's no lady," he muttered wryly, "that's my wife."

2

Huh?'' The salesman's mouth went slack with surprise. He bit down on his cigar stub just in time to keep it from falling out. He must have been familiar with the old burlesque joke that Drew had cracked, but one look at the lethal smile that went with it told him that Drew wasn't joking. "Your . . . wife?"

"Ex-wife," Andra corrected archly.

Drew turned his lethal smile on her. "Not yet."

"Did you hear this?" With a bitter croak of a laugh, the salesman turned toward the table where the other players were still busy counting up their winnings or losses. "His wife just happened to be standing in back of me with a reflecting pocketbook!"

"*Ex-wi—*" Andra started to insist before she saw Drew's reaction.

His black eyes narrowed dangerously, and every

powerful muscle in his body stiffened. "Are you accusing my wife of being a distracter?" he asked carefully. Either he couldn't believe that he'd heard the man correctly or he was making sure that he had before retaliating.

"It's probably just a coincidence that he didn't start to win until *she* showed up," the salesman continued in a loud, outraged tone of voice calculated to attract everyone's attention again. The crowd, which had begun to disperse, slowed and looked back toward the railing.

"If you've got something to say, why don't you say it to me?" Drew ordered with a deadly calm that managed to sound far more menacing than his opponent's blustering anger.

The salesman hesitated for a moment, aware that he'd gone too far but unable to stop himself. The sense of threat, which Andra had glimpsed behind his friendly facade, was all too evident now. His thick hands balled into fists. Compared to Drew's long, elegant hands, his were the size of ham hocks. Like Drew, he was six feet three and had seventy or eighty pounds on him; most of it was fat, while Drew was all taut, sleekly toned muscle. But it was the venomous look in the man's eyes that frightened Andra. She'd never seen such naked rage.

"Drew, please," she implored. Too late she remembered that Drew was not the kind of man to back down when he knew he was right.

"It's okay, love," he said softly, reassuringly, but the determined glint in his eyes demanded that she trust his judgement. It was the unconscious use of the old endearment, the way it sounded as if he still meant it, that shocked Andra into acceptance.

Turning, Drew confronted the salesman head on. "Are you accusing me of using my wife to cheat?"

The entire room went silent. In Vegas, cheating was considered a more serious crime than murder. Andra was aware, once again, of the electric charge in the air, that undercurrent of danger. The crowd was hurrying back to the brass railing, excitement junkies eager for another fix.

Pausing in the middle of counting up Drew's chips, the casino cashier motioned to a giant of a man leaning up against the mahogany bar across the way. He might have been waving to a friend, his gesture was so casual. The plainclothes guard pushed away from the bar and headed quickly in their direction.

"Are you accusing me of cheating?" Drew repeated grimly.

The salesman set himself, ready to throw the first punch. "You got to admit you didn't start winning until *she*—"

"Leave her out of this!" Drew cut him off. "I didn't start winning until I got a fresh deck of cards." He slanted a glance at the plainclothes guard, who was now leaning against the inside part of the railing. A look passed between them. Drew knew that the guard was allowing him to handle the situation and was acting as backup in case things got out of control. The man had quickly read the salesman as the potential threat to the well-ordered fantasy his employers worked so hard at creating, and he never took his eyes off him.

Drew turned to the cashier, who was still counting up chips with the speed and accuracy of a computer. "Pete, why don't *you* check those cards to see who's cheating around here," he said coldly. "Let's check the first deck too, while we're at it."

The salesman's face darkened and veins popped out on his thick bull's neck. Andra thought that he was on the verge of an attack of some kind. Instead, he broke into one of his raucous laughs. "Who said anything about cheating?" His hands went limp and he staggered back a few steps as though all the bourbon he'd had to drink had finally gotten to him. "Did any of you guys ever once hear me mention the word 'cheating'?" he inquired of his playing partners in the pathetic tones of a totally misunderstood individual.

"You could have fooled me," Drew drawled sarcastically.

"Why don't you go and sleep it off, Eddie?" the urban cowboy suggested with a trace of disgust.

"Would you like someone to see you to your room, Mr. B.?" the cashier asked with practiced solicitude.

"Nah, I'm okay. I guess I jus' drank a bit much," he mumbled, his words getting more slurred by the minute. "And losin' all that money . . ."

"If you can't lose gracefully, you shouldn't play the game," Drew said flatly.

A wistful smile flickered across Andra's face. Drew really didn't belong in this city, she thought wryly, or in this century. He should have been a riverboat gambler on the Mississippi, when his kind of pride and chivalry still had meaning. It bothered her that she couldn't help being proud of him.

"Who lost?" The salesman laughed raucously again, but there was a hard edge to it. "Consider that money a loan. I'll get it back tomorrow night—and then some."

The compulsive gambler looked up from the marker for two thousand dollars that he was in the middle of signing. "Does this mean the tournament's still on?" A ray of hope flared in his desperate, bloodshot eyes when he turned them on Drew.

"Same time, same place," Drew said.

"Great. See ya all then." The salesman was about to take off when Drew stopped him.

"Aren't you forgetting something?" he asked dryly.

"What's that?"

"I think you owe the lady an apology."

The "lady" found herself the center of everyone's curious attention. This time, Andra silently cursed Drew's out-of-date chivalry.

"Oh, sure." A big, friendly grin split the salesman's beefy face as he staggered over to Andra. There was a malicious little gleam in his beady eyes. He was not as drunk as he pretended. "Sorry, little lady." He made a mocking attempt at a bow. "I didn't mean no harm. But a gambler's wife," he chided patronizingly, "should know better than to go to a casino carrying a shiner."

Dismissing her abruptly—like most gamblers he clearly considered women mere momentary distractions—he turned his attention back to Drew. "See ya tomorrow night." He pointed a stubby, diamond-ring-studded finger at him. "I'm gonna wipe you out."

He laughed loudly again, as if it were all in fun. Something in his tone frightened Andra even more than his rage had before. She was sure that he'd literally meant what he'd said. She was suddenly afraid for Drew. Her fear was mixed with resentment. Why did he have to live this way, surrounded by this kind of people?

It was not her problem anymore, she reminded herself irritably. It was over. Finished. Tomorrow, the last remaining link between them would be severed for good.

With a final mocking bow, the salesman went on his way. At the other poker setups, games resumed, and the crowd split up into single lonely units again. Looking lost and somewhat let down, they straggled out into the main section of the casino, hoping to find some action in there. Andra sighed audibly with relief.

"Are you all right?" Drew asked with genuine concern as he stopped by her side. She'd forgotten how overwhelming his presence could be up close, and it threw her for a moment. She was grateful for the cashier's interruption.

"How do you want this, Mr. R.?" he asked politely, a look of obvious respect on his lean, sharp features. "Cash? A check? Or would you prefer that we held it in the cage for you?"

"Why don't you do that, Pete? I'll need it tomorrow night. Just let me have a thousand in cash."

"Certainly, Mr. R." The cashier bowed his head respectfully. "I'll get your receipt." He hurried off toward the cage with the metal racks of chips as the other players exchanged quick good-byes with Drew before going off in search of fresh excitement.

"I'm sorry about . . . all that," Drew said when they were alone again. "You sure you're all right? You seem a bit upset."

Andra shrugged it off. "I guess I'm just not used to all this anymore," she said wryly. "I haven't had this much excitement since the last time I saw you."

"I'm glad to hear it." He grinned when he saw that the double meaning in his words had not been lost on her. "Sounds as if you're leading a rather boring life these days."

"No. But I'm sure *you* would think so," Andra parried coolly. "While I find this just a bit too much excitement for one evening."

"The evening isn't over yet." A suggestive smile played on his lips, and his eyes gleamed with wicked humor.

"I've had enough excitement for one night, thank you."

"Too bad," he drawled huskily as his gaze glided over every curve of her body, remembering.

Once again, Andra was grateful for the cashier's timely interruption. "Here's the cash you requested, Mr. R." He handed Drew a packet of brand-new hundred-dollar bills neatly circled with a paper band marked $1,000.

Drew slid a crisp bill expertly off the top of the stack and offered it to him. "Thanks, Pete."

"Thank *you*, Mr. R." The hundred-dollar bill disappeared with one flick of his fingers. As if he were a magician performing a trick, it was replaced by a slip of white paper. "And here's your receipt for your winnings." Just before he took off for the cashier's cage, he added as an afterthought, "It comes to $52,000."

Drew glanced absently at the receipt before thrusting it, along with the cash, into a special zippered compartment inside his jacket.

Andra couldn't resist a teasing smile. "I'm glad to see that your luck has changed."

"You know what they say, 'Lucky at cards, unlucky at love.'" Andra was taken aback by the bitter sarcasm in Drew's tone. He turned his head away from her abruptly. When he turned back, he had his poker face on. "Let's get out of here. Let's go someplace where we can—"

"Look, Drew," Andra objected. "I didn't come almost three thousand miles to help you celebrate your big win."

"That's nothing to celebrate," he returned shortly as he started for the swinging doors.

"But I know how much you love to celebrate a big win," she reminded him. "It was always so important to you."

Drew shrugged with a kind of bored disgust. "Not anymore." Andra was speechless. She remembered only too well how after a big win Drew would be on a high for days. "I just want to get out of here," he muttered, "and go someplace where we can talk."

He paused in front of the swinging doors when he saw that Andra was hesitating. He couldn't know that it was because she was wondering what could have caused this change in him. He was afraid that she was having second thoughts about having a drink alone with him. "You do want to settle this divorce thing once and for all," he asked dryly, "don't you?"

"Yes . . . of course," Andra murmured haltingly. "That's why I came to Vegas."

"Then let's do it." Drew held one half of the swinging doors open for her. He smiled sardonically. "After you, Mrs. Ramsey."

Mrs. Ramsey stifled an exasperated sigh as she walked past him into the main gambling area of the casino, her high heels sinking into the plush puce carpet.

"Did you have a good flight?" Drew asked conversationally as they made their way through the dice pit past the gamblers tossing murmured incantations onto the crap tables along with the glittering red dice.

"Yes. It was fine."

"Did you have any trouble finding me?"

"No. You wrote that you'd be playing at this hotel." A rueful smile tugged at the corners of Andra's mouth. She'd learned very early on in the course of their two-year marriage where to look for Drew. She couldn't resist adding, "It didn't take any great detective work on my part to locate the nearest high-stakes poker game."

Drew slid her an undecipherable look.

The crowd was five deep around the roulette tables, eagerly waiting for someone to relinquish a seat. Andra had to raise her voice to be heard over their murmuring and the sound the silver balls made whirling around the roulette wheels. "There seems to be a mix-up with the reservations you booked for me."

"No mix-up," he assured her. "I've taken care of everything."

"But the desk clerk said there was no . . ."

"Don't worry about it," Drew insisted as he suddenly wrapped his arm around her back. Andra jumped at his touch. If he noticed it, he gave no indication. Instead, he tightened his hold and guided her firmly down the carpeted steps leading to the blackjack pit.

"I knew you'd hate staying in one of the hotels on the Strip, so I made other plans for you," he explained when he released her.

There was a sudden, awkward tension between them.

Andra could still feel the imprint of Drew's arm through the lightweight fabric of her dress, the spot of warmth where his fingers had curled around her waist. It surprised and annoyed her that Drew's touch, as casual as it had been, could still affect her. He seemed oddly subdued.

In total silence, they made their way through the blackjack pit past the double row of horseshoe-shaped tables, the flash of blue-backed cards on either side.

When they negotiated their way through the army of one-armed bandits standing in formation at the front of the casino, Andra was grateful for the silver shower of coins systematically hitting the holders. The specially made metal coin holders made the winning of a dozen quarters sound like a jackpot of hundreds, and the sound filled the awkward silence between them.

Andra was positive that the elderly women playing the slot machines—a coin-filled paper cup in one hand, a padded workman's glove on the other—were the same ones she'd seen the last time she was in Vegas. The sight depressed her as much as it had almost a year before.

Although it was nearly one A.M., the Friday-night

crowd was still pouring enthusiastically into the casino, filling the aisles. Anyone coming from the opposite direction, as they were, had difficulty trying to get out. Drew moved ahead of Andra, one hand gripping her wrist, the other stretched out in front of him as if he were Orpheus leading Eurydice out of hell.

3

Andra let herself out of Drew's silver-toned Maserati before he was able to get around the sleek sports car to open the door for her. She stopped short when she recognized the converted carriage house he'd just parked in front of. The brass plaque bearing the name Delacroix's still reflected the amber glow of the antique lampposts flanking the heavy oak door.

"Why here, of all places?" she demanded.

"It's quiet . . . no tourists." Drew shrugged matter-of-factly. "And we won't have to shout to be heard over the slot machines."

That wasn't what she'd meant. Andra knew that Delacroix's was a popular Vegas hangout where professional gamblers and nightclub entertainers could go to unwind after a long day's night. But it had also been *their* favorite hangout when she and Drew were still living together. She had more memories of the evenings they'd spent there than she cared to remember. She was sure that was why he'd chosen it.

"There must be someplace else we can go," she said coolly, shifting unconsciously from one foot to the other.

She always did that when she felt unsure of herself, Drew recalled, as if the very ground under her feet was unsteady. That was one of the things about Andra that had first intrigued him—the vulnerability under the calm, self-assured manner.

"Offhand, I can't think of one. It's where I always go when I want to relax," Drew said, keeping his face and voice as expressionless as when he was running a heavy bluff. "Of course, if you feel you can't handle it . . ." He let his voice trail off and waited for her inevitable reaction. She would have to call his bluff, he assured himself, she was too proud to do otherwise. His palms were damp.

"I guess it's as good a place as any," Andra said with a proud toss of her head. "Let's just get it over with." Turning, she walked resolutely to the entrance. Pulling the heavy oak door open, she stepped quickly inside. The sense of déjà vu was instant and overpowering.

The dinner club was exactly as Andra remembered, casually elegant and inviting. She'd always found the decor—exposed brick walls, burnished oak floors, and beamed ceilings—a welcome relief from the baroque gaudiness of the typical Vegas establishment. It was the only place that she knew of, in that relentlessly illuminated town, where the lights were kept low. The authentic gaslight fixtures, with their delicately etched crystal bowls, gave off a warm, amber glow that added to the intimate ambience. Burgundy velvet banquettes were grouped in such a way as to insure privacy.

The dance floor where she and Drew had danced away many a night was empty. The musicians were obviously on their break, since they'd left their instruments on the bandstand.

Andra and Drew both stopped automatically in front of the cloakroom. They waited there side by side for the maître d', who was already on his way over to them. For the second time that evening, Andra had the odd sensation that nothing had changed, that they were picking up exactly where they'd left off.

"Monsieur Drew! What a great pleasure it is to see you and your lovely bride once again." The maître d's round, pink face positively glowed. He stood there for a moment, beaming up at both of them, since even Andra, at five feet seven, was taller than he. "But it has been too long," he scolded paternally.

"Thanks, Emile." Drew returned the dapper little man's smile sincerely. "It's great to be back."

Andra shot Drew an accusing look, which he ignored. He'd just led her to believe that he was still a frequent patron.

"I hope you do not mind, Monsieur Drew," the maître d' went on in his charmingly accented voice while he escorted them to a table, "if I tell to Madame that she is looking more beautiful than before?"

"I don't mind," Drew said directly to Andra. "I couldn't agree with you more."

"Thank you, Emile," Andra managed politely.

"*Et voilà.*" With a sweep of his dainty hand, the maître d' indicated the corner table he'd led them to. There was a conspiratorial twinkle in his large, soulful eyes when he added, "I have your favorite table for you."

Andra groaned inwardly. That was all she needed: another dose of déjà vu.

"Is this all right, love?" Drew asked when he saw her hesitate. His look was all concern, pure innocence. She could have kicked him. "Would you rather sit somewhere else?"

"It's all the same to me." Andra gave what she hoped looked like a bored shrug. "This is fine, Emile."

"*Très bien, Madame.*" Turning his head, he quickly scanned the table. With his dainty fingers, he fastidiously smoothed out the tablecloth and readjusted the flower centerpiece. When he was satisfied that everything was as it should be, he whipped a cardboard sign off the table and slipped it into his pocket.

Andra hadn't gotten a good look at it, but she could have sworn it was a Reserved sign.

With an elegant sweep of his hand, Emile invited her to sit down, indicating the side of the banquette with its back to the rest of the room where she and Drew always sat. The booth was large enough to seat four, so they used to sit side by side rather than across the table from one another.

Nodding her thanks to the maître d', Andra slid into the other side of the banquette.

Drew's mind registered her action, but his face remained impassive. "Thanks, Emile." He folded a ten-dollar bill into the maître d's hand before he slipped into the opposite seat.

"*Merci*, Monsieur Drew." The man bowed his head slightly. "I will send your garçon *tout de suite*. So good to see you both again." The smile he flashed at them

35

before he hurried off to seat another party was warm and sincere.

Drew sank back against the upholstered banquette with a wry smile. "Just like old times."

"Not quite," Andra reminded him sharply. They weren't newlyweds any longer. They were there to discuss the final details of their divorce. It annoyed her that he could make light of it. "And I wish you wouldn't look at me that way."

"I'm sorry. I didn't mean to stare, but I haven't seen you in almost a year," he said politely and continued to stare. "A lot can happen in a year."

Andra was surprised by the uncharacteristic tone of insecurity in Drew's voice, which he was quick to cover up. "You look great. I must confess, I was secretly hoping you'd be pale and gaunt . . . just wasting away for want of me," he added with a typically sardonic smile. "Instead, you've never looked lovelier."

"Well, you're looking as dashing as ever," Andra countered. She had to make an effort to keep her tone as brittle as his, to make light of how disturbingly attractive he still was. "You haven't changed at all."

But it wasn't true. There was something different about him and she didn't know what it was. Something in his manner, in the depths of his eyes. He was thinner, she noted again, his face unusually pale and drawn. It couldn't have been "for want" of her, she assured herself; he'd probably stayed up all of the night before playing poker. And, if anything, it added to his dark, dramatic looks, giving him a slightly haunted look that, she was sure, most women would find irresistible.

"I like it," Drew said, cutting into Andra's thoughts.

"Excuse me?"

"Your new hairdo," he explained, eyeing the soft ash-blonde waves that framed her face and curved just under her chin. "I like it."

Andra's hand flew to her hair self-consciously. "No, you don't. You always liked it long." She laughed suddenly. "Remember how angry you were that time I wanted to get it cut?"

"It's not *that* short," Drew murmured, his gaze moving over her hair like a caress. "I could still sink both hands into it."

Andra's eyes widened and her lips parted in shocked surprise at his comment and the memories it evoked. For a moment, she reexperienced the sensation of his long, sensitive fingers coiling in her hair. "I knew I should have gotten a crew cut," she got out tartly.

"Ahh, Monsieur Drew . . . and Madame. So nice to have you back!" exclaimed Claude, the waiter who usually served them. A grin of genuine pleasure lit up his boyishly handsome face. "We have all missed you."

Andra sighed irritably. She was beginning to feel that there was a conspiracy going on.

"Thanks, Claude. We've missed being here." Drew shot Andra an ironic look. "Haven't we, love?"

She shot back a speak-for-yourself-John glare.

"May I get you a cocktail?" Claude asked, pen and order book at the ready.

Drew nodded and turned to Andra. "Would you like a drink?"

"Yes, please."

"Two extra-dry vodka gimlets on the rocks?" the waiter anticipated—it was their usual order.

"No, not for me," Andra said, which caused him to stop writing and wiped the pleased smile off his face. "I'd rather have a glass of white wine."

"Ah, *oui*, Madame." He scratched out the entry. Reaching over, he picked up the gold-tassled wine list and offered it to her. "A bottle . . . half a bottle?"

"Make that a bottle of champagne," Drew ordered casually.

"Oh, no," Andra protested. "All I want is a glass of wine."

"That's all champagne is . . . wine with bubbles," Drew said teasingly. "I'll share it with you. Claude, make that a bottle of Dom Pérignon . . . '78 if you have it."

"Ahh, a special occasion," Claude murmured knowingly while he made a note of the order.

An ironic smile played on Drew's lips and in the dark depths of his eyes as they locked with Andra's. "In a way."

Andra waited until the waiter was out of hearing range before sending Drew an ironic smile of her own. "You're the only person I know, Drew, who could turn a divorce into a special occasion."

"You always said that I was like no one else." Without taking his eyes off her, Drew reached into his inside pocket for his gold cigarette case and lighter. "You claimed that was one of the reasons you loved me."

Andra carefully replaced the wine list in its silver filigree holder. "I'm amazed that everyone still remembers us," she said.

"How could they not remember us?" Drew's voice was a husky murmur. "This isn't exactly Niagara Falls. In Vegas they're not used to the sight of newlyweds acting like a couple of love-struck kids."

The memories Andra had been trying so hard to suppress flooded her mind. "We certainly did carry on," she was forced to admit. Picking up one of the menus, she opened it and held it up in front of her. The menu was so large it successfully hid her face from him. They used to sneak kisses behind it, she suddenly remembered.

Andra closed the menu and placed it back on the table. "What time is our appointment tomorrow?" she managed to say coolly. "Or should I say, later today?"

Drew took a moment to light his cigarette. "What appointment?"

"With the lawyer," she reminded him. "Or do we have to go to court? I'm not sure what the procedure is here in Nevada."

"I told you, I've taken care of everything," he said smoothly. "That was part of the deal. All you have to do is sign the papers."

"But if we don't have to discuss the details of the divorce," she demanded impatiently, "what are we doing here?"

Drew took a long, hard drag on his cigarette and stared at Andra silently for a moment. He exhaled harshly. "I thought we might discuss the reason *why* you want a divorce."

"Drew, you *know* why." Andra sighed painfully. "Please, we've been through all this before, so—" She was unable to continue. Claude was on his way to their table, an ice-filled wine cooler in one hand, a bottle of Dom Pérignon and a pair of fluted glasses in the other. Neither of them spoke while the waiter went through the ritual of chilling the bottle of champagne with a flourish.

Andra could feel Drew staring at her with that same intensity with which he calculated the odds on his winning a game. She continued to ignore him. She wasn't playing the game his way any longer.

Drew took a long, impatient pull on his cigarette. He was having trouble reconciling the Andra he remembered with the one who was sitting across the table from him now.

So cool, he noted, so cool, calm, and collected. And still achingly lovely. He felt the tension start to coil inside him. She could still do that to him, he realized with a mixture of surprise and annoyance. Just looking at her could still do that to him.

Andra turned her head abruptly toward the unmistakable sound of live music that had just started up from the bandstand. With what was rapidly turning into a terminal case of déjà vu, she recognized the musicians. She tried to block out the memory of the times she and Drew had danced to their music, but it was too strong. She could have kicked herself now for letting her pride get the better of her and allowing Drew to bring her there.

She never would have believed that the memories could be so vivid or have such an effect on her. The soft, bluesy music was affecting her already strained nerves. It took every bit of willpower that she possessed to appear outwardly calm.

Drew took a drag on his cigarette before he realized that he'd smoked it down to the filter. He wondered if

Andra was thinking about the times they'd danced there together and if it meant anything to her. It bothered him that he couldn't reach out and touch her the way he used to, the way he wanted to. He wanted to break through her cool reserve, to see her the way she had looked the last time they'd been together: her face flushed, her hair in wild tangles, her delicate body shaking in his arms as he made love to her.

Drew squashed the filter tip out in the ashtray. No emotion, he warned himself, just stick to the plan.

He went back to studying Andra objectively. Her attention was now fixed on Claude, who was having trouble working the cork out of the bottle. She seemed oblivious to Drew's presence. She was deliberately ignoring him, he decided. He watched as she shifted almost imperceptibly in her seat. She wasn't as cool and composed as she pretended to be either.

The champagne cork finally popped with a deafening bang, causing Andra to gasp with excitement. The bubbly liquid foamed over the top of the bottle, spilling onto the tablecloth. She laughed, as delighted as a child, and her gray eyes sparkled while they watched Claude quickly pour the champagne into the glasses. The coil inside Drew tightened another notch.

Claude slipped the champagne bottle into the silver wine cooler. "Enjoy your evening," he said to them with an openly suggestive grin. The smile froze on Andra's face. There was an awkward moment of silence after the waiter hurried over to a party who'd been signaling him.

Reaching for his fluted glass, Drew raised it in a mocking toast. "To our divorce."

"I'll drink to that," Andra returned in kind. Drew

was deliberately toying with her, she realized as she clicked glasses with him. What damn game was he up to now—and why?

She took several sips of champagne. It was delightfully dry and bubbly, but her mind was on more important matters. With wide, serious eyes, she peered over the rim of her glass at him. "Drew, why did you make my coming to Vegas a condition for granting me a divorce?"

"Since you walked out on the marriage," he told her wryly, "I felt the least you could do was be there for the divorce."

Andra shook her head sadly. "I didn't think what we had *was* a marriage."

"Well, I did."

"I know. That was the problem."

Drew gave Andra the strangest look, then canceled it out with another mocking smile. "Why did you accept my condition?"

"Because it would have taken me a year to get an uncontested divorce in New York."

Drew took a long, thoughtful swallow of champagne. A bit of sparkling foam clung to the bottom edge of his moustache. He licked it off with the tip of his tongue. "Are you sure that's the reason?"

Andra uncrossed her legs and shifted in her seat. "Of course. What other reason could I have?" she insisted defensively. "As a Nevada resident, you can get a no-fault divorce in a matter of weeks."

"What's the rush?" He twirled the stem of his champagne glass ever so casually. "Have you met someone else?"

"No, of course not," Andra blurted out. She was

instantly sorry that she had. She didn't need to remind him that he was a tough act to follow. Next she'd be telling him how she'd been unable to date other men.

"So what's the rush?"

"I want to get on with my life, Drew," Andra said impatiently. "I can't go on living in limbo—not really married, not really free." She tugged a stray lock of hair behind her ear. "I want to be free."

Drew's fingers tightened around the stem of his glass. A bitter smile twisted the corners of his mouth. "After what we've had together, do you actually believe a piece of paper is going to set us free?"

Andra's hand froze in midair as she was about to take the last sip of her drink. It wasn't just what he'd said—which was disturbing enough—but the way he'd said it. It was the first emotion he'd shown since they'd begun discussing the divorce. She suddenly had the feeling that everything they'd been talking about was sheer nonsense. Something else was going on behind Drew's sardonic facade.

Andra set her glass down and waited for Drew to finish polishing off his champagne so she could face him. "Why am I here, Drew?" she asked evenly. "What do you want from me?"

Turning away from her, he smoothly slid the bottle of champagne out of the wine cooler. "What makes you think I want something?"

"Because I know you. I know how your mind works." She held her glass up automatically to make it easier for him to refill it. "I've watched you play poker too many times not to recognize a bluff when I see one."

Drew cursed himself silently. He'd let his feelings for

her almost wreck his game plan. If he wasn't careful she'd read him like a marked deck. She was the only person he'd ever known who could. He'd never let anyone else get that close.

He finished refilling his glass and then slid the empty bottle upside down into the bucket. "I don't know why you feel that way, Andra."

"Drew, don't bluff me. This isn't a poker game, it's life . . . my life." Her voice was unsteady, her eyes deeply troubled. "The one thing you never did was play games with *me.*"

"That's true," he muttered, as though he regretted it now. He tapped his long fingers on the table twice with that staccato rhythm he used whenever he checked at poker. "But you're on the other side of the table now."

"I see." Andra took several careful sips of champagne. It seemed to have lost its sparkle. "So now *I'm* included in that long list of opponents that you feel compelled to face and beat."

"It does say Ramsey versus Ramsey on those papers," he pointed out caustically.

"It also says no-fault." It hurt Andra that Drew considered her an enemy now—more than she would have believed possible. "Drew, neither one of us is to blame because the marriage didn't work out," she rattled on compulsively. "We should never have gotten married in the first place. We're just not . . . right for each other."

"You could have fooled me," he muttered into his glass.

"I tried . . . I really did try to be the kind of wife that you needed," she went on with difficulty, "but—"

"I never had any complaints," he cut her off shortly. "You're the one who left me, remember?"

Once again, real emotion flared in his voice and eyes, as startling as a flash of lightning in a clear summer sky. It was gone just as quickly. It stirred up the guilt feelings that haunted Andra whenever she thought about the way she'd left Drew. Telling herself that he'd given her no choice didn't help—maybe it would if she told *him*.

One look at the hard, stubborn set of his jaw and the words of explanation, which she'd rehearsed in her mind countless times, shriveled up inside her. Once Drew shut himself off behind that poker-faced mask of his, she knew there was no reaching him.

She watched him coolly light up another cigarette and cursed that damn, stubborn pride of his. That's all it was, Andra assured herself, hurt pride. If he really loved her, he'd have tried to save their marriage. He hadn't even made an attempt to come after her and bring her back.

"You want to . . . punish me for leaving you," Andra murmured, verbalizing the thought that had just occurred to her. "That's why you insisted that I come back here, isn't it?"

Drew took a drag on his cigarette and gave Andra a long, bemused look.

"Drew, you promised that if I came to Vegas," Andra got out miserably, "you wouldn't make things difficult."

"I'm sorry." He exhaled a stream of smoke. "I didn't mean to spoil our friendly divorce."

Andra shook her head with a defeated sigh. "There's no point in going on with this." She suddenly felt exhausted. "Since we obviously have nothing constructive to say to each other, I'd like to leave now."

Surprise flickered in Drew's eyes, but his face and voice remained indifferent. "Aren't you going to finish your champagne?"

"No, thanks." With a shaky hand, Andra pushed her glass away. It was almost full, but she couldn't have swallowed another drop. "It's been a very long and trying day. I'd really like to go now." Grabbing her patent leather bag from the table, she fumbled with the metal chain that functioned as a shoulder strap.

"All right," Drew agreed reluctantly. "Let me get the check." Spotting Claude, who'd just finished serving a party several tables away, he made the appropriate signal. "Then we'll drive straight to—"

"Don't bother," Andra interrupted him. Giving up trying to unkink the twisted metal links of the chain, she slung it over her shoulder the way it was. "I'll get a taxi to take me back to the airport." She got to her feet quickly and rather clumsily. "I should never have come here."

"Andra, don't!" Reaching across the table, Drew grabbed her hand to hold her back, but it was the uncharacteristic pleading in his eyes that stopped her. "Please, don't."

"But there's no point in—"

"Yes, there is," he insisted, tightening his hold as she sought to free her hand from the strong, warm crush of his. "Okay, I'll tell you why I insisted that you come to Vegas."

Caught off balance physically as well as emotionally, Andra grabbed the edge of the table with her free hand. She was sure that this was just another one of Drew's ploys, but when she looked at him again, his eyes were the darkest she'd ever seen them.

"I need your help," he said tightly.

Andra's hand went limp in his. She no longer doubted him; she knew him too well. Drew's pride had never allowed him to ask anyone for help, not even her.

"Are you in trouble?" she asked anxiously. The image of their friend Paul lying in bandaged pieces in a hospital bed flashed in her mind. Andra sank back down in her seat. "Bad trouble . . . like Paul?"

"No, nothing like that." Drew squeezed her hand reassuringly. He grinned. "But it's nice to know that you still worry about me."

Andra didn't know whether to be relieved or furious. Feeling a combination of the two, she pulled her hand away. "Then what is it?"

"It's not something we can discuss in a few minutes . . . or in public," Drew said pointedly as Claude set the silver tray with the check down in front of him. He put his cigarette out and waited until they were alone again before going on. "That's why I couldn't tell you about it before." Checking the bill with one hand, he reached into the special money compartment inside his dinner jacket with the other. "I'd rather talk about it after we've both had a good night's sleep."

Drew was aware that Andra was beginning to study him warily again. He knew that he couldn't afford to give her time to think; he had to keep her off balance.

He quickly paid the check, leaving Claude an absurdly generous tip so they wouldn't waste any time waiting for change.

"If you still want me to take you to the airport, I will," he told Andra with the cold-blooded nerve of a gambler who knows that he's got the best hand in the game but checks to keep the others from dropping out. "I understand if you'd rather not get involved."

"No, I'd be glad to help . . . if I can," she said sincerely. She only wished that he'd asked for her help before, not now that it was too late.

"Thanks, love." He gave her a warm, devastating smile. It went right through her. Getting quickly to his feet, he graciously offered his hand to help her out of the booth. As if on cue, the band segued into a lush, romantic melody.

"I don't believe that. They're playing our song," Drew said as though he couldn't be more surprised. His hand closed around hers. "How about a dance?"

"You've got to be kidding," Andra gasped as she found herself being maneuvered smoothly to the dance floor.

"Come on, Andra, they're playing it just for us. We can't disappoint them," he insisted lightly. "They obviously think we're still madly in love."

And, in fact, the quartet of musicians was looking at them with the most nauseatingly sentimental smiles on their shaggy-haired faces. From his station in front of the cloakroom, the maître d' was beaming at them with soulful eyes.

"You don't want to destroy everybody's illusions, do you?" Drew added sardonically as he eased her onto the deserted dance floor.

There was no way that Andra could get out of dancing with Drew at that point without making a scene. She sighed, exasperated. "I'd forgotten what an impossible man you are."

"I haven't forgotten anything about you," he murmured provocatively as he pulled her into his arms.

Andra stiffened automatically, anticipating the sudden hard contact with his body. Instead, Drew held her lightly in the conventional dance pose. She relaxed. Falling into step with him, she moved effortlessly to his rhythm and the sensuous strains of the disturbingly evocative melody.

He *would* be wearing her favorite cologne. And it was having its usual effect on her. Without meaning to, she breathed in the spicy fragrance that went so well with the tangy scent of his skin. Memories flooded her mind and senses, blurring the boundary between past and present.

Andra started counting the number of pleats on Drew's shirt front. The way he was holding her, she could feel the tantalizing brush of his thighs against hers, the tips of her breasts grazing his chest with every movement. She lost count somewhere around pleat number six.

"For two people who aren't 'right' for each other," Drew muttered dryly, "it's remarkable how perfectly we fit one another."

Another crack like that, Andra promised herself, and she'd kick him right in the shins. "It takes more than physical compatibility to make a good marriage," she shot back, her body following his effortlessly into a turn. "Unfortunately, that's all we ever had."

"Had?" he ground out derisively. His arm tightened

around her, pulling her hard against the strong, taut length of his body. He smiled when he felt the shiver that went through her. His hand slid down to the small of her back to press her hips intimately against his. Andra gasped as she felt him hard and warm through the layers of clothing. "Had?"

She tried to find an appropriately scathing reply but couldn't; she couldn't have voiced it if she had. She could barely breathe from the rush of emotions and sensations that were coming alive inside her. She was stunned that he could still have such an effect on her.

Andra knew that she should pull back from Drew again. She told herself that she was going to. But it had been so long since she'd known the pleasure of his arms around her, the warmth of another body next to hers. All the loneliness and emptiness of the past year, which had settled into her bones like a permanent chill, were beginning to thaw. In a kind of daze, she pressed her body closer to his, eager for the healing warmth of him. While the sensuous music drifted around them, she closed her eyes, letting her head fall onto his shoulder.

The muscle in Drew's shoulder contracted, and he missed a step when Andra's body melted softly against his. The hunger for her widened inside him. He could have taken her right there on the spot. Drawing in a long, steadying breath, he warned himself not to overplay his hand. He'd found out what he'd wanted to know: he still had the power to seduce her physically. But that hadn't stopped her from leaving him before. This time, he was going to have to seduce her mind, body, and soul.

Andra's eyes flickered open. She struggled to break

through the sensuous daze she was caught up in, which was rapidly becoming a deep, aching hunger. Before she could recover, Drew lowered his face to hers and slid his cheek against her temple.

"You know, Andra, you were always wrong about one thing," he whispered thickly, his warm breath caressing her skin, clouding her mind again. "You always believed that I loved you because sex was so fantastic with us . . ." He paused to nuzzle her ear. His moustache tickled, sending tiny shivers down her spine. "But the truth was, sex was so fantastic with us *because* I loved you."

Drew released Andra abruptly before she could hide the impact his words had made on her. A victorious look gleamed in his eyes as they swept over her flushed face and trembling body. "Do you still think a piece of paper is going to set us free?"

Andra staggered back several steps. Her shaking hands clenched into fists at her sides. She was a split second away from giving Drew that kick in the shins he so richly deserved. That would certainly give everyone in the place something to remember them by. But she refused to give him the satisfaction of knowing that he could still affect her so deeply.

His sardonic grin informed her that he was already aware of that fact. "Are you sure you don't want to reconsider getting a divorce?"

"As a matter of fact, I *am* reconsidering divorce." She smiled at him ever so sweetly. "I'm seriously beginning to consider murder." Sweeping past him, Andra left Drew standing in the middle of the dance floor.

4

‿∾∾∾∾∾∾∾∾‿

As Drew slipped behind the wheel of the Maserati, Andra closed her eyes and let her head fall back onto the padded headrest. The long, difficult day had finally gotten to her; she no longer had the strength to deal with Drew. Dancing with him had left her more shaken than she cared to admit, even to herself. She was sure that if she spoke so much as a word she'd give herself away.

Mercifully, Drew assumed that she was a victim of jet lag and took the hint. He silently maneuvered the sleek sports car into traffic.

With an unconscious sigh of relief, Andra let herself sink mindlessly into the glove-leather softness of the bucket seat, lulled by the hypnotic purr of the motor. But as tired as she was, she was in no danger of falling asleep. Even with her eyes closed, she was intensely aware of Drew's body next to hers. She reexperienced the sensation of being held in his arms, the impact of being crushed against the long, hard length of his body.

A shiver went through her and she shifted in her seat. With every bit of willpower she possessed, she forced her mind to go blank. But the warm, tangy scent of him continued to swirl around the edges of her consciousness.

The sense of too much time gone by, too much distance traveled for what should have been a relatively short trip to whatever hotel Drew had booked her into, finally forced Andra's eyes open. For a moment, all she could do was blink dumbly through the windshield at the vast, black emptiness the car was speeding toward.

Jerking her head around, she looked out the rear window and saw the glittering lights of the Strip, a winding, multicolored python of neon, receding further into the distance. Puzzled, Andra looked over at Drew.

The strong, jagged line of his profile was barely visible against the black-leather-upholstered interior of the car, which reflected no light. Not that there were any lights to reflect along the barren highway leading out of Vegas. He appeared unaware of her movements, but she knew better—nothing escaped his awareness.

What was Drew trying to pull now? Andra wondered irritably. The thought that suddenly occurred to her was too outrageous even for him.

Andra peered through the windshield again. Accustomed to the darkness now, she was able to make out the outline of the mountains that circled Las Vegas. Just as she'd thought: Drew was driving straight for the desert.

"Drew, where are we going?" Andra demanded, as though her mind were incapable of accepting the information her eyes were clearly supplying.

"Hi." He slid her a friendly grin before turning his attention back to the road. "Did you have a nice nap?"

"Are we going home . . . I mean, to the house?"

"Yes, of course," he said. He sounded amazed that she would have to ask. "You know you'd hate staying at a hotel on the Strip," he added before she could protest, "and why spend all that money when the house is available?"

"And where will *you* be staying?" she asked pointedly.

"At the house—where else?" He shrugged nonchalantly. "You don't think I'd leave you out there all alone?"

Andra bolted upright in her seat. "Drew, I have no intention of spending the night under the same roof with you."

"It may be the same roof, but it'll be different sections of it," he drawled wryly. "You can sleep in the bedroom, and I'll take the guest room."

"No!" Andra shook her head violently. "Absolutely not."

"What's the problem?" He seemed truly perplexed by her attitude. "Don't you trust me?"

Andra laughed in spite of herself, a short, sardonic laugh.

Drew shook his head ruefully. "I can't imagine what

I could have done to make you distrust me," he murmured with just the right trace of hurt in his tone.

"How about leading me to believe that you'd made a reservation at a hotel for me and then pulling *this* stunt?" she inquired dryly.

"I never said I'd made reservations at a hotel," Drew protested, all innocence. "I told you I'd made other plans."

"You just neglected to tell me what they were."

"We never got around to talking about it. I never dreamt you felt this way." He slanted her a deeply sincere look. "I thought you'd rather stay at the house. You always loved it there. That's the only reason I bought it . . ." He let his voice trail off wistfully.

Andra sighed, exasperated. She'd relived enough for one night. She couldn't even begin to handle being alone with Drew in the same house.

"Drew, will you please turn this car around," she said carefully, trying to keep her voice steady, "and take me back to Vegas? I'll get my own room."

"Andra, it's after two A.M. on a Friday night," he reminded her. "There isn't going to be a decent room available in that whole town without a reservation, you should know that."

"Damn," she cursed under her breath. "How could I have been dumb enough to let you make reservations for me?"

"I'll drive you back to Vegas if you really want me to," he said patiently. "But we're going to spend the rest of the night driving around looking for a room." As if to prove his point, Drew indicated the weekend traffic that was zipping along the opposite side of the highway, still pouring into Vegas at that ungodly hour.

"I will not stay in the same house with you," Andra cried angrily, feeling trapped and helpless. "I'll sleep in the car first!"

"Suit yourself," Drew said pleasantly as he smoothly executed the turn onto Route 39, which winds through Kyle Canyon.

"You think I'm kidding."

"Oh, no, I don't," he muttered sincerely. His brain was already working double-time trying to find a way to talk her out of it. The success of his game plan depended entirely on getting Andra to stay in the house with him.

"I bet you think you're pretty clever," Andra went on caustically, "the way you set this whole thing up."

Drew seemed totally absorbed in negotiating the deserted, winding road, but he was deliberately letting Andra blow off steam while he studied her out of the corner of his eye. Years of playing against the toughest pros in the business had made him an expert on human behavior. He was able to decipher an opponent's true frame of mind from the slightest inflection in the voice, the most disguised bit of body language, and then use that knowledge to his advantage.

"Well, it's not going to work," she assured him coolly. "I'll sleep in the desert with the damn coyotes before I sleep in that house with you."

"You would too, wouldn't you?" Drew glanced over at Andra with an openly admiring grin. Even in the dim light from the dashboard, Andra's eyes glowed, bright with determination. She looked tired, and she knew that she was cornered, but she held her head up proudly. Only her bottom lip gave her away—it trembled slightly, soft and vulnerable.

Instinctively, Drew made his move. "What are you afraid of, Andra?"

She stiffened defensively. "I'm not afraid."

"Like hell you're not," he taunted. "Are you afraid of me? Do you think I'd try to force myself on you?"

"No, of course not," she admitted grudgingly. She knew from experience that Drew had far more persuasive methods.

"Then you're obviously afraid to trust yourself with me in such a . . . potentially intimate situation."

That was closer to the truth and Andra knew it, but she wasn't about to admit it. "I see your ego has gotten a few sizes larger since the last time I saw you."

"*My* ego?" With a sharp laugh, Drew snapped his head around to stare at her. "What about *your* ego? You're the one who's assuming that I'm trying to lure you up to the house to seduce you." He shrugged his indifference. "Why would I want to seduce you?"

"What?"

Drew swung the car over to the side of the road and braked it before turning in his seat to face Andra. "Why would I want to seduce you?" he repeated as if it was the most ridiculous thing he'd ever heard.

"Well, why else would you have set it up so that I'd be forced to stay at the house alone with you?"

"I told you, I thought you'd rather stay at the house than at a hotel," he explained reasonably, patiently. "But obviously your ego can't accept that explanation."

"My ego has nothing to do with it!" Andra practically shouted, furious at him for twisting everything around.

"Andra, I really didn't mean that as a put-down,"

Drew drawled soothingly. He leaned toward her. "You're lovelier and more desirable than ever." Narrowing eyes locked hard with hers. "But do you think I could forget what happened the last time I made love to you?"

The memory of their last night together suddenly came alive between them. Drew caught the flash of guilt in Andra's eyes and it gave him a jolt of satisfaction. The raw pain the memory evoked in him came as a surprise, sharpening his tone to a cutting edge. "Do you actually believe that I'd put myself in a position where you could do that to me again?"

All the fight went out of her; just drained right out of her like the blood from her face. She turned away from his bitter, accusing look and stared blindly out the side window.

"Do you?" Drew bit out with more emotion than he'd intended. The game he'd set up so carefully was suddenly turning real on him, and he had to fight to keep control of it. Reaching out, he cupped Andra's chin and turned her exquisite face back to his. "There's only one way I'd ever touch you again, love," he vowed thickly. "If you begged me to." His thumb grazed her jaw, softly traced her startled lips. "But you wouldn't do that, would you?"

Andra's head snapped back, her eyes shining with tears she refused to shed. "No, never."

A perverse little smile twisted Drew's lips, as if he'd anticipated her answer. He sat back up in his seat. "In that case, you're as safe with me as with your maiden aunt."

Releasing the brake, Drew swung the car back onto

the road. He drove the last two miles to the house without so much as a word or a look at Andra.

"That's all you brought . . . one suitcase?" asked Drew with a perplexed frown when he pulled Andra's overnight bag out of the trunk of his car where the bellboy had stashed it on his orders.

"I'm only staying a couple of days," Andra reminded him pointedly. Ignoring his deepening frown, she reached past him for the two hard leather cases: one contained her camera; the other, various photography equipment.

"You *did* bring a camera," Drew murmured, shutting the trunk.

Andra detected a note of satisfaction in his tone, but she couldn't for the life of her understand what might have caused it. She was too tired to try and figure it out. Not bothering to stifle a yawn, she nodded affirmatively. "Force of habit, I guess."

She slipped her head through both leather straps, anchoring her precious equipment against her body. She didn't realize that the crisscrossed straps pressed the fabric of her dress tightly against her breasts, emphasizing them, until she caught Drew staring.

Her right hand went up to tug at the strap on her left shoulder, her arm attempting to cover her breasts. Drew smiled. The ironic look he shot her reminded her that he'd already seen, touched, and tasted every inch of her body—and remembered every bit of it. Then, turning away from her abruptly, he walked over to the entrance.

Andra hesitated, stopped by the rush of memories

the sight of the house evoked in her. She'd fallen in love with it the moment she saw it. Built from tawny sandstone, limestone, and boulders—materials taken from the desert—the contemporary structure gripped and echoed the stark landscape surrounding it. Wall-sized windows welcomed stunning views of the multi-colored desert into every room of the house. The two-story-high cathedral ceiling reached up toward the endless sky like a prayer.

A feeling of irretrievable loss swept over Andra when she saw the For Sale sign hanging from an arm of the giant cactus standing prickly guard beside the door.

She followed Drew inside the house and was hit by the biggest jolt of the evening. Everything was exactly as she'd left it, the exact way she'd decorated it. Not one ashtray was out of place.

"Do you still remember the way?" Drew inquired sardonically when he started upstairs to where the bedrooms were located. Andra didn't answer. She wished that was all she remembered. She stopped dead just before they got to the master bedroom.

"Uh, I'll sleep in the guest room, Drew," she said, trying to sound casual. "After all, I am the guest."

"You'll be much more comfortable in here," he insisted politely as he carried her overnight bag inside.

"I'd rather sleep in the guest room." Andra had to stick her head into the bedroom to be heard. "Really, I would."

"But I've already moved all my things in there, Andra. Here . . ." Drew bent over and pulled the top drawer of the dresser open; it was empty. "You see?"

"Yes, I see," she muttered wryly. "I guess I'll sleep

in here, then." She waited in the doorway, making it clear that she had no intention of going into the bedroom as long as he was in there.

A bemused smile tugged at the corners of his mouth as he came over to her. "I'm right next door if you need anything."

"I won't need anything," she assured him sweetly.

He shrugged good-naturedly. "I'm there if you want me," he tossed over his broad shoulder as he started down the hall.

5

〜⌒⌒⌒⌒⌒⌒⌒⌒〜

Andra locked the door behind her and surveyed the bedroom she'd decorated with such loving care. It was her favorite room in the house because it most completely captured Drew's personality. Pale yellow walls gave the spacious room a light, cool look and set off the black lacquer-and-brass Oriental furniture dramatically. Black lacquer also framed the antique Japanese screen hanging over the bed, a fantasy landscape done in gold leaf that shimmered like molten gold. The bold, masculine look of the furnishings was softened by the sensuous elegance of the pale yellow satin bedspread and drapes, the buttery wall-to-wall carpet.

Everything was exactly as she'd left it, except for the two dozen yellow roses on the night table next to what used to be her side of the bed. Normally, Andra would have been pleased by Drew's lovely gesture, but she had the gnawing feeling that it was all part of some devious plan of his.

She stopped her restless wandering in front of the corner vanity table. Wistfully, she reached out and touched the faded pink organdy dress of the Kewpie doll that still dangled from the bamboo cornice of the mirror. She laughed softly as she remembered how Drew had won it for her in Atlantic City the night they first met.

With a muttered curse at herself, Andra turned away abruptly, and moved on to the dresser, only to find that she'd left the Kewpie doll behind but not the memory.

Her breath caught in her throat, just as it had the first time she saw Drew. Having always been a sensible, both-feet-on-the-ground type of person, Andra had never believed in love at first sight—until she had looked up from the slot machine she'd been feeding quarters into and seen the tall, devastatingly attractive stranger staring at her with the darkest, most intense eyes she'd ever seen.

She couldn't remember how she'd managed to talk her parents into letting her spend Memorial Day weekend in Atlantic City with her cousin Emily. She recalled only the excitement she'd felt at being away from home for the first time.

Andra couldn't help smiling at the painfully shy, naïve twenty-two-year-old she'd been. How she'd longed to break free of her restrictive, overprotective upbringing. Even then she'd felt that there had to be more to life than being a Long Island matron like her mother, who lived only to impress the other country club matrons and was totally subservient to her husband. The Judge, as Andra's father was called even at home, was a devoted, dependable family man, and she was sure that he loved her in his way. His way was not to show it.

Andra ran her long, delicate fingers over the camera she'd just set carefully on top of the black lacquered dresser next to the lenses.

Until she married Drew, her photography had been the only thing in her life over which she'd dared to oppose her father's wishes. The Judge felt that photography was not a suitably refined profession for a woman. No matter how hard she tried, she was unable to make him understand how much it meant to her, how she longed to explore the world around her, to freeze time and capture luminous pieces of life forever. She wouldn't have dared to tell him that she intended her life to be meaningful and exciting. She couldn't have known, as she boarded the bus for Atlantic City, that she was about to find more excitement than she could handle.

As Andra started getting ready for bed, she reexperienced the rush of warmth that had gone through her, the way her mouth went dry when the tall, devastatingly attractive stranger came over to introduce himself.

She'd never known a professional gambler and was hopelessly intrigued. Before the evening was over, she realized that she'd never met anyone like Drew Ramsey—and never would again. So when he graciously offered to be her guide to the Monopoly-board city, as he called it, she eagerly accepted.

As inexperienced as she was with men, Andra knew

instinctively that Drew had fallen as hard for her as she had for him. Being a sensible young woman, however, she was sure that all he felt was a purely physical attraction. She was also fully aware of the danger, as well as the sheer stupidity, of getting involved intimately with a man she'd never see again once the holiday weekend was over.

Slipping out of her silky bra and panties, Andra dropped them on the chair on top of the rest of her clothes. She shook her head, smiling in disbelief. Even from the mature, objective distance of four years, she found it difficult to believe that shy, well-brought-up Andra, both-feet-on-the-ground Andra, the-last-virgin-in-her-class Andra, had been willing to go to bed with a man she'd known only three days!

She froze at the head of the bed—her skin still remembered the feel of his, the taste of him was still in her mouth.

Andra took several deep breaths as she resolutely turned down the bed covers and tried to make her mind go blank. But the bed held more insomnia-provoking memories than anything else in the room. The last time she'd seen Drew was when he'd made love to her in that bed.

That was the last thing she should be thinking about! she told herself miserably. With a groan of self-disgust, she slid between the ivory satin sheets. The groan became a gasp. She was sorry now that she'd been too tired to unpack a nightgown. It had been a long time since she'd slept in the nude or between satin sheets. She'd forgotten how incredibly sensuous it could be. She shivered uncontrollably.

At first, Andra thought it was just a reaction to the

feel of cool satin against her heated skin. When she couldn't stop shaking, she realized that it wasn't so. She was shivering deep inside, just as she had that first time she'd gone to Drew's hotel room.

With a painful sigh, Andra let her head fall back onto the pillow, shutting her eyes tightly against the memory invading her mind and senses. She shivered uncontrollably again. . . .

"You're shivering," Drew murmured thickly as he reluctantly dragged his mouth away from hers. He'd barely closed the hotel room door behind them when he pulled her into his arms, kissing her over and over again, deep, devouring kisses that left her shaking uncontrollably. "I wasn't too rough with you, was I?"

"Oh, no," she managed breathlessly but she couldn't stop shaking. When her eyes flickered open, the room was swaying around her and she had to dig her fingers into his shoulders to steady herself. She never knew that you could get drunk on kisses.

"I'm so hungry for you," he breathed against her trembling lips, punctuating his words with hungry little bites of her mouth. "I've wanted to . . . kiss you like that . . . from the first moment . . . I saw you." Strong, all-encompassing arms tightened around her until the soft curves of her body gave way to the muscular hardness of his and she could feel every part of him. "I don't know how I've managed to keep my hands off you . . . until now."

Andra gasped as the tip of Drew's tongue traced the outline of her lips and tasted their inner softness again, sending another wave of hot chills shivering through her. Before it could plunge deep inside her as before, arousing feelings and sensations she'd never known, still hadn't recovered from, she pulled her head back.

"Andra?" His eyes narrowing with concern, Drew searched her face. Something glimpsed in the dazed depths of her eyes made him ask, "Are you sure you want this?"

"Yes," she moaned, "oh, yes." The only thing she *was* sure of was how much she wanted him. Everything else that was happening was so new and overwhelming, even frightening. She could feel the blood rushing through her veins, throbbing at every pulse point in her body. Her heart was smashing against her rib cage one moment, barely beating the next. She was dizzy with love for him, totally vulnerable and defenseless.

"It's just . . ." With a ragged sigh, Andra buried her face against Drew's chest. She could feel his body heat right through his clothes and was amazed to find that his heart was pounding as erratically as hers. It gave her the courage to explain why she'd hesitated. "It's just that I've never . . ."

"Andra, you don't have to say anything," Drew murmured, his breath warm and unsteady on her hair. "I know a woman like you doesn't make a habit of going to bed with a man she barely knows."

She didn't make a habit of going to bed with a man, period—that's what she'd been trying to tell him!

"Or in a place like this," Drew went on disgustedly, indicating the hotel room's imitation Louis XIV decor, all gilt and white baroque furnishings, tassled canopy bed and mirrored ceiling. "I know everything happened so fast . . . but it happened to both of us."

He slid his hands into the long, tangled silk of her hair to draw her face back to his. "This is all very new to me too," he said softly, unsteadily, his eyes like molten midnight. "I've never felt like this about any women I've ever known."

Andra's eyes widened and she stopped breathing.

"It sounds like a line, I know," Drew admitted with a crooked smile. "I bet others guys have said that to you before, but . . ."

"Oh, no." She shook her head, sending her pale, baby-fine hair spilling over his hands. "No one else has ever told me that . . ." She was about to add that there had never been anyone else, but Drew bent his head and brushed her lips softly with his, his moustache tickling, sending a tiny shiver through her.

"No matter what happens, I want you to believe that," he pleaded intensely. "I've never felt this way before . . . ever."

"What . . . way?" She didn't know how she got the words past the lump in her throat.

"Just very . . ." He paused as if the experience was so new to him, he couldn't find words to describe it. His long, sensitive fingers tightened in her hair. "Come here," he whispered thickly, "let me show you." His mouth took hers again in a long, slow, achingly tender kiss.

With a broken moan, Andra wrapped her arms around Drew's neck and she went all open to him—her mouth, her body, her deepest self. She was stunned by the intensity of her response and his reaction, and all she could do was cling to him as he kissed her breathless.

"That's what I meant . . . I never knew kissing

could be so damn sexy," he got out raggedly when he came up for air. "I've never wanted to just kiss someone like I do you." His hands uncoiled in her hair to move searchingly down her body. "I'd love to kiss every delicious inch of you."

Andra gasped as Drew's words and hands sent a kind of fearful excitement spiraling through her.

"And I love this blouse on you," he murmured huskily, "It *is* you." His hands glided down the front of her high-necked antique lace blouse, over the softly rounded curve of her breasts, in a lingering caress. "So fine and delicate."

Drew took Andra's pulse with his lips when he unbuttoned each frilly cuff. Every time his expert fingers undid one of the tiny pearl buttons running the length of her blouse, he dropped a kiss on her exposed skin. When he was through, there was a series of warm, wet dots where the buttons had been.

Andra held her breath as Drew caressed the blouse off her shoulders and down her slender arms and back. With one sudden, impatient flick of his fingers, the fastening of her skirt came undone. Making a sound like a drawn-out sigh, the silky fabric shivered down her long legs to the carpet.

The breath Andra finally released came out in pieces. Fear and excitement shot through her again as she stood before Drew in only her bra and panties. All she could think of was how she longed to be beautiful for him. When she found the courage to look at him, she was stunned by what she saw reflected in his eyes—no woman could be that beautiful.

When Drew realized that Andra was watching him,

he shook his head with a self-conscious grin. "You make me feel like a sixteen-year-old with his first girl," he murmured. "Christ, I didn't act this way when I *was* sixteen." He went down on one knee before her to retrieve her skirt. "But then, I was never sixteen." His fingers hesitated, seduced out of their original intent by the sensuous feel of the silk, the pull of old memories. "I was already hustling for a living with my father, and we moved around so much, I never had a girl." The memories swept over him, darkening his face, edging his tone with wry bitterness. "Only one-night stands, semipros . . . never a girl of my own."

He looked up at her then, regret twisting the rugged lines of his face as if he expected her to be completely turned off by what he'd said. She wasn't.

Only love and a deep sadness—for the boy who'd never had a girl, the man who'd never been a boy—suffused Andra's face. She reached out and smoothed a stray lock of hair off his forehead. "I'll be your girl," she said on the wisp of a breath.

"Yes, be my girl," he pleaded fiercely, reaching up for her as he went down on his other knee. "My fine . . . beautiful girl." Wrapping both arms around her waist, he buried his face between her breasts, crushing her to him as though he meant to make her part of him.

Shaking with emotion, Andra wound her arms around Drew's neck, holding him close and hanging onto him at the same time. The tremor that went through his powerful body took her completely by surprise, reverberated inside her like the rippling waves of an aftershock. Wave after wave broke over her, taking her breath away, as his mouth moved hungrily over her breasts, burning right through the lacy covering of her bra.

Andra staggered back a step when Drew's hands suddenly released her to glide up her back. She never felt the hooks of her bra being undone, only the cool feel of nylon as it slid down her heated skin, making her gasp. With a purely reflex action, her arms came up to cover her naked breasts, but they couldn't hide the embarrassing blush creeping up her neck and face.

Surprise stopped Drew cold and narrowed his eyes; then they softened with understanding—and an emotion that Andra was too shaken to be able to decipher. "Don't be ashamed," he murmured tenderly. "You're too lovely to be modest." His hands moved to capture her wrists. Softly but firmly he spread her arms wide open. His breath seemed to catch in his throat at the sight of her, then rushed out as his melting gaze glided over her naked breasts with the impact of a caress. "Much too lovely," he rasped just before his mouth closed over the tentative bud of a nipple.

Andra cried out at the startling intimacy of his kiss, the burning tug of his mouth splintering her with pleasure. Drew made a sound deep in his throat as he felt her nipple harden against his tongue. His hands released her wrists to rush down her body. When impatient fingers hooked onto the edge of her panties to tug them off, Andra cried out again and pulled back involuntarily.

Drew's hands fell to his sides as he stared up at her with growing amazement. "Andra," he got out with difficulty, "this isn't the first time for you . . . is it?"

Andra tried to answer, to say something witty or

sophisticated, and hide the excruciating embarrassment she felt, but all she could do finally was nod.

A curse hissed out of him and he sat back on his heels. "Why didn't you tell me?"

"Well, I . . . I tried to, but," she stammered, feeling more naïve and foolish by the second, "but what difference does it make?"

"What difference does it make? Jesus Christ!" Reaching for her skirt, Drew started pulling it back up her legs.

"What are you doing?" Andra cried, pushing it back down.

"Andra, put your . . . put your skirt back on," he stammered.

"I don't understand. Why?"

"Why?" With a determined tug, he got the skirt past her hands and over her hips. "Because you can't give yourself for the first time to someone like me," he said miserably as he fumbled the fastening of her skirt closed. "That's why!"

"Why not?"

"Because," he said through gritted teeth, scooping her bra off the carpet. "Because someone like me is here today, gone tomorrow."

"I know that," she said clearly, proud of herself for sounding so mature. "I know I'll never see you again after tonight"—her voice would go and crack on her!—"but it doesn't matter. Drew, I want you to make love to me."

"Here." Getting to his feet, Drew held the bra up to her in a no-nonsense manner. His hand was shaking. "Come on, put this back on."

"No! Drew, I know what I'm doing," she protested

as he grabbed her arm to slide it through one of the straps. "I know that tonight is all we'll have together. That's why I don't want to waste it."

"Will you stand still?" he bit out between clenched teeth while she kept flailing her arms about to keep him from putting the straps on.

"You don't understand, I love you," she cried angrily. Because of his superior strength, she was unable to stop him from getting her arms through the straps. The bra dangled from her elbows when she threw her arms impulsively around his neck. "I've never been in love before . . . I don't know if I ever will be again."

A groan that was half a curse tore out of him as he tugged the bra into place. "Look, one day you'll thank me for this." His hands went around her back, but only to hook up her bra.

Andra used the opportunity to press her body closer to his. She felt powerful muscles tauten against her, and he let loose with another groan-curse. She began, "Drew, I . . ."

"One day," he went on, his voice raw, his fingers struggling with the hooks, "when you meet the right man for you, then you'll . . . dammit!" His hands gave up in frustration. "I'm not any good at putting these damn things *on*!"

"Then don't!" She shrugged out of the bra. Longing for the feel and warmth of him, she pressed closer. "And even if you're right and I do meet someone else someday . . . I still want . . . " To hide the blush that was spreading over her again, Andra buried her face in the hollow of Drew's shoulder. "Oh, how can I make you understand?" She sighed as she felt the pulse beating erratically under her parted lips. "Drew, I want *you* to be my first lover."

She heard his sharp intake of breath and felt his whole body contract; then his arms locked around her in a fierce hug. He held her for an endless moment, murmuring something unintelligible in her hair. Then his hands slid abruptly to her waist and he pushed her away, breaking the loving bonds of her arms.

"I can't do it," he got out raggedly. "I can't make love to you, knowing that it's your first time and . . . " Stepping back with a harsh sigh, he raked a shaky hand through his hair. "And then get on that plane back to Vegas tomorrow . . . and just leave you like that." He shook his head, looking as amazed by his behavior as she was. "I just can't do that."

"But I told you," Andra began, taking a step toward him.

"Don't." Drew held his hand up to stop her as though he knew that if she took one more step he would be unable to resist her in spite of his good intentions. Black-as-midnight eyes moved over her half-naked body with a combination of longing and regret. "Please get dressed," he said through clenched teeth, "or I'll . . ."

Turning away from her abruptly, Drew stalked over to the complimentary bar. "I think I could use a drink right about now." He tried to smile, but it came out lopsided. "How about you?"

Afraid to trust her voice, Andra shook her head. Blinking back tears, she concentrated on keeping her hands steady as she began dressing. She reminded herself that, in spite of the way she'd acted that evening, she was a sensible young woman who'd been brought up to not make a spectacle of herself. There would be plenty of time for tears after Drew was gone.

The silence between them was broken, magnified, by the sound of ice cubes hitting against the side of Drew's glass when he drank and the sharp expulsions of breath when he exhaled as he chain-smoked while he waited for her to finish dressing.

The silence was complete during the elevator ride down to the sixth floor where Andra's room was and while Drew escorted her down the long, winding hallway that smelled of hotel disinfectant.

Andra was vaguely surprised by how calm she was when she unlocked the door to her room. She felt only that emptiness that she'd always thought was a normal part of life—until this weekend with Drew—and a strange constriction just under her heart, a heaviness, as if she were carrying her love for him inside her stillborn.

"Did you mean what you said before?" asked Drew suddenly, just as Andra was about to step through the open door.

"What?" She'd said so many things, most of which she knew she should regret but didn't.

A wry smile tugged at the corners of his mouth. "You said you loved me."

"Oh, that." She laughed, a painfully constricted little laugh. "I know it sounds crazy, but I . . . yes, I do."

"Enough to come back to Vegas with me?" he asked, his voice neutral.

"You want me to go back home with you?" she asked incredulously. The tears she'd put off filled her eyes, turning them to burnished silver, and a glow suffused her face. Eagerly she blurted out, "You mean . . . tomorrow?"

"No, not tomorrow," Drew answered wryly. "You're going to need time to get your things together, straighten everything out with your parents and . . . " He paused as he saw the light go out of her eyes.

"My parents," she said miserably. She looked like a child who'd been given a wonderful gift only to have it snatched away.

"Would it help if I went home with you?" Drew offered. "I could meet them, talk to them."

She shook her head hopelessly. "You don't know the Judge—my father."

"The Judge?" he repeated dryly. No further explanation was needed. He went very still in that intense way that he had when he played poker. He seemed to be weighing his odds, trying to decide whether to stay or drop out. "Okay," he said finally, easily, "then let's get married."

Andra's mouth opened, but no words came out.

"I meant what I'd said also, Andra. I've never felt like this before. I don't want to lose it." He reached out to trace her startled face softly. "Five'll get you ten I won't get this lucky again."

"Oh, Drew!" She threw herself into his arms, planting a wet, crooked, and very noisy kiss on his mouth.

"This, I take it, is your answer?"

"Yes . . . yes . . . yes!" she cried ecstatically, dropping tiny kisses all over his face.

"Hey, hold up." He laughed under her delightful assault. "Don't you want to think about it?"

"Think?" she said. She'd forgotten what that was. She hadn't had a sensible thought all weekend and she'd never been happier in her life—why spoil it? "You didn't have to think about it; why should I?"

"But I'm a gambler," he reminded her seriously. "I'm used to making big decisions in a matter of seconds. I make a living trusting my instincts."

"Oh?" she said teasingly. "And just what did your instincts tell you this time?"

He didn't return her smile. Instead, he looked deeply into her eyes. "That you're the kind of woman a man could stake his life on," he said with a certainty that struck her speechless again. "But I want *you* to think about it carefully."

"I have instincts too," she said softly but proudly.

"Just sleep on it, as they say, okay? You can give me your answer at breakfast tomorrow."

"Okay," Andra agreed, but her answer was already shining in her eyes and all over her face. When Drew saw it, he grabbed her impulsively, pulling her up against the long, tautening length of his body, and his mouth came down hungrily on hers. He groaned deep in his throat when he felt her instant, total response to him.

"I'm going to love being married to you," he said hoarsely against her mouth. "But unless you want to consummate this union right here in the hallway, you'd better get out of here." With a warm, sexy laugh, he pushed her inside her room. "Sleep well and . . ."

"Sleep well!" Andra muttered with angry sarcasm as she shifted restlessly between the satin sheets. She hadn't fallen asleep until dawn that night, and it looked as if she wasn't going to fall asleep at all this night, thanks to him again.

With a muffled curse, she rolled over onto her stomach and then onto her side, but no matter which way she turned, she couldn't get comfortable. The king-size bed was too large; she felt lost in it.

She punched the pillow viciously, squashing rather than fluffing it up.

It's over, she reminded herself angrily, finished! By this time the next day they would be divorced; she would be free of him and she'd finally be able to sleep again. She couldn't understand why she was crying.

Burying her face in the squashed pillow, Andra reached blindly for the dimmer switch on the night table and turned out the light.

Drew's head shot up when the rectangle of light spilling through the glass doors of the master bedroom went out, plunging the rest of the balcony into total darkness. The reading light he'd left on in the guest room wasn't bright enough to reach the corner of the balcony where he was sitting.

He felt a definite twinge of satisfaction when he checked his digital watch; it glowed 3:28. He was glad that he wasn't the only one having trouble sleeping. So far, the cards were falling exactly as he'd stacked them. Knowing how sensitive Andra was, he'd counted on her remembering the last time she'd been in that bed and how he'd made love to her.

Lighting another cigarette from the butt of the one he'd just smoked, Drew wondered whether Andra ever thought about that night. Heaven knows, *he'd* never been able to get it out of his mind. He must have gone over it a few hundred times in the past year, taking it apart and putting it back together like the strategy of a game he'd lost, trying to find out where he'd gone wrong.

He cursed himself as he always did when he thought about that night and took another slug of vodka. He should never have left her to go to that damn poker game, even if it was the championship tournament. But he was so sure of her, so sure that after making love to her until she was shaking uncontrollably in his arms, until she clung to him as if she were coming apart, she wouldn't be able to leave him as she'd threatened.

"Stupid, arrogant idiot!" he exhaled along with a bitter stream of smoke. He'd almost gone crazy when he got home later to find her gone, a hastily scrawled note pinned to the sheets still tangled from their lovemaking.

A sharp pain twisted Drew's guts, just as it had that night and every night for the next week when he came home expecting Andra to be there again. A bitter rage replaced the pain when he finally realized that she wasn't coming back. If she could live without him, he vowed, if she could forget everything they'd shared those last three years, then he damn well could too.

He moved out of the house and back to a hotel on the Strip, back to his old life. Before he'd married Andra, he lived like a gypsy—ever since he was a kid bumming around the country with his father, a penny-ante pool hustler; he'd never known his mother. His home became a hotel room again, just a place to shower and change, to sack out or shack up. He went back to eating in restaurants, when he remembered to eat. And he did everything he could to forget her. He went out with other women, gambled recklessly, drank more than he ever had in his life. None of it worked.

Squashing out the cigarette almost viciously in the ashtray, Drew leaned his head back and rotated it slowly, trying to work out the kinks in his neck.

He was finally forced to admit how much he'd changed because of Andra. How much he looked forward to coming home to her, the dinners they shared, going to sleep and waking up wrapped around her. She was the only woman he'd ever been able to talk to, the only one he'd ever shared things with. After being with Andra, the women he was used to seemed harder and cheaper than before. He stopped going with them. And for the first time in his life, gambling lost its thrill. Even when he won big, he felt like a loser without her.

Drew took another long, hard gulp of his drink. It burned his already nicotine-raw throat. An ironic smile twisted his mouth. He'd already decided to swallow his pride—a seven-course meal if ever there was one—and go to New York after her when he got the letter from her lawyer about the divorce. It was like losing her all over again, but it strengthened his determination to win her back.

He let the letters and phone messages from her lawyer pile up over the next few months until he was ready to make his move. He went about winning Andra back the only way he knew how—as if she were a game of high-stakes poker. He calculated the odds, worked out a foolproof strategy, and did the one thing he'd never do in a real game—he stacked the deck. The next day he would spring his ace in the hole.

Half-melted ice cubes hit against Drew's teeth; they were all that was left of his drink when he tried to take another swallow. He was tempted to make himself another vodka on the rocks. He sure as hell could use it. Only the discipline he'd acquired over the years as a professional gambler stopped him and brought him to his feet.

He was determined to keep his head clear, his senses sharp, as he always did before a big game. The next day he was going to play the most important game of his life, he reminded himself as he slid the glass doors open and stepped resolutely into the guest room to get ready for bed. It was the one game he couldn't afford to lose.

Uttering a soft little cry in her sleep, Andra turned over onto her side. Reaching out, her hand searched the satin emptiness beside her. In her dream, the petals of the yellow rose she was clutching disintegrated in her hand.

6

~~∽○○○○○○○○○○∽~~

"Good morning," Drew called out cheerfully, moving with long, sure strides through the maple-paneled entrance to the kitchen. The same reddish blond wood lined the counters and trimmed the cream-colored cabinets and walls, giving the narrow but ultramodern kitchen a warm glow.

"Good afternoon," Andra corrected with a smile, since it was well past noon. Lifting the omelet pan from the burner, she gave it one last shake before giving Drew a quick, sideways glance. Rather, she'd meant to give Drew a quick, sideways glance, but it got stuck. The photographer in her couldn't resist the picture he made.

She'd always had a weakness for black and white photography and Drew made a devastating study. His thick black hair, bushy eyebrows and moustache, and midnight-dark eyes contrasted dramatically with the stark white of his skin. She'd never seen a man combine virility with elegance quite the way he did. He looked as bold as the black and white stripes of his silk shirt, as sharp as the knife pleats in his white linen trousers.

Andra snapped the picture mentally, adding it to the indelible collection in her mind, before she remembered how important timing was in the preparation of an omelet.

"Whatcha cookin'?" Drew joshed on his way over to her. Andra kept her attention fixed on the omelet she was carefully rolling over to the other side of the pan with a fork. Only after she had it resting successfully on the lip of the pan did she reply. "A stuffed omelet."

"Looks like one of your superduper ones. What's in it?"

"You should know." She smiled wryly. "You bought the ingredients." She hadn't been surprised to find he'd remembered her favorite brunch. She was coming to realize that it was all part of a carefully thought-out plot. What she still hadn't figured out was what Drew hoped to achieve. With a curt nod of her head, she indicated the half-filled bowl on the counter next to the stove. "Smoked ham, Fontina cheese, and sautéed mushrooms."

Andra wasn't aware that Drew was standing directly in back of her, peering over her shoulder, until he leaned his head forward. "Mmm, sure smells good. You're making my mouth water," he growled hungrily. "And the omelet's not bad either." He laughed, a low, sexy laugh, and his warm breath brushed the side of her cheek.

Her hand slipped and the fork pierced the omelet, making a rip in it. Melted cheese began oozing out, but she managed to flip the omelet onto the heated plate without causing further damage. Irritably, she wondered why the hell he was in such a good mood that morning.

Andra couldn't have known that the sight of her in T-shirt and jeans, cooking for him as she used to, filled Drew with a childlike joy. It was a sight he thought he'd never see again.

Sliding the plate with the omelet back under the warming hood next to a platter piled high with toasted bagels, Andra turned and pointed her fork at Drew's chest. "Don't mess with the chef."

"Yes, ma'am," he agreed playfully, putting his hands up as if she were holding a gun on him. "But what does a poor starving hombre have to do around here to get one of them thar omelets?"

"Just give me some room, pardner," she returned, trying to keep things light between them because the kitchen suddenly seemed too narrow and confining. "This here kitchen ain't big enough for the both of us."

"I know someplace that is," he drawled with a suggestive grin, but he backed off, stepping over to the refrigerator. "Was the bed comfortable?" he inquired casually, pulling open the door to the freezer compartment. "You didn't have any trouble sleeping, did you?"

"No, not at all," she lied coolly. The fresh butter she was swirling around the omelet pan wouldn't have melted in her mouth.

"Yeah, that sure is a great bed." He sighed—there

was a world of memories in it. "I've always enjoyed . . ."

"What are you doing?" Andra cut him off sharply, indicating the bottle of imported vodka he'd just removed from the freezer.

"Making us Bloody Marys," said Drew, clearly amazed that she would have to ask. He always made Bloody Marys at brunch. "Is it okay?"

"Fine." Andra shrugged her unconcern and practically demolished the egg she was in the process of cracking against the edge of the stainless steel bowl.

The familiar ease with which they were going about their respective tasks, their bodies adjusting automatically to the narrow space and to one another, unnerved her—and made her wreck the other egg.

Reaching over Andra's head to get the spices he needed from the upper cabinet, Drew asked cheerfully, "So what would you like to do today?"

"Do?" She shot him a wary look while she finished picking bits of shell out of the egg mixture. "What do you mean, do?"

"It's such a beautiful day . . ." With a disarming smile, he nodded toward the sunlight streaming through the high window that framed a clear, almost painfully brilliant desert sky. "It's a crime to waste it indoors." As he slid a can opener out of the bottom drawer, his arm brushed hers.

The sensuous feel of silk and the living warmth beneath the silk raised goose bumps on Andra's bare arm. "Yes, it is a beautiful day," she agreed, beating the eggs into a frenzied froth. "A perfect day for a divorce."

As though he hadn't heard her, Drew punched two

holes in the top of a can of tomato juice and then slipped the opener back into the drawer. Continuing over to the freezer, he got several ice cubes out of the automatic ice-maker and plopped them into the waiting glasses.

"And while we're on the subject," she persisted, pouring the overly beaten eggs into the pan, "where are the papers?"

Drew took his time pouring vodka over the ice cubes. "What papers?"

"The divorce papers," she reminded him dryly. Why did she have the feeling that she also needed to remind herself of why she was there? She gave the pan a good, hard shake to keep the eggs from sticking to the bottom and almost sent the still runny mixture spilling over the edge. "The ones I'm supposed to sign?"

"Oh, those papers," said Drew. He paused to count the drops of Tabasco sauce he was adding to the Bloody Marys. "They're at my lawyer's."

"Your lawyer's?" Andra's fork, which should have been gently prodding the thickening omelet to keep it cooking evenly, froze in midair. "But I thought you said last night that—"

"Sorry, love," Drew interrupted, "but would you pass the salt if you're through with it?"

Stepping away from the stove with a wary frown, Andra carried the saltshaker over to Drew. "Last night you said that all I had to do was sign them. That we didn't have to go to the lawyer's."

"We don't." Salting the drinks, he slid her a reassuring smile. "He's coming here."

"He's coming here?" she repeated incredulously on her way back to the stove. She gave the frying pan another good shake, but the few moments she'd let it out of her hands were enough to make the omelet stick to the bottom in unevenly cooked lumps. Reaching for a spatula in a last-ditch effort to save the omelet, she asked, "When?"

"Sometime Monday afternoon," Drew tossed over his shoulder on his way out of the kitchen with the drinks.

"Monday afternoon?" Andra wailed. Reaching over, she slid open the window in the pass-through counter between the kitchen and the dining room. "Drew, I'm booked on a flight back to New York Monday morning," she protested as he came into view. "You'll have to make another appointment."

Drew finished setting the Bloody Marys on top of the woven straw place mats on the table. "Unfortunately, I can't do that, Andra."

Having given up on saving the omelet, Andra quickly dumped the ham, cheese, and mushroom filling into the pan, scrambling everything together. "I'm almost afraid to ask," she muttered sardonically, "but why can't we make another appointment?"

"Because my lawyer's away for the weekend," he told her breezily.

"What?" Andra scraped the eggy mess onto a plate and slammed it down next to the omelet and the bagels. "But you knew that I was flying in this weekend just to get the divorce."

"True," he agreed amiably, silverware flashing out of his long, elegant fingers as quickly and efficiently as if he were dealing out cards. "But I didn't know that he would be flying out." With an ingenuous smile, he stepped over to the pass-through counter to pick up the platter piled high with toasted bagels. "He's taking his kids to Disneyland."

"Disneyland? Perfect!" Andra threw her head back with a sarcastic laugh. "The perfect place to get this Mickey Mouse divorce." She stormed out of the kitchen and into the dining room.

Having removed the plates from the counter, Drew was standing in front of the table, smiling quizzically down at the one with the scrambled egg mess. One look at Andra's face wiped the smile off his, but a wicked remnant twitched the corners of his mouth and gleamed in his eyes. "I see you made a *frittata*."

Drew never knew how close he came to wearing a *frittata*—or maybe he did, because he quickly set the plate on the table just as Andra was reaching for it. Setting the one with the omelet down on the other place mat, he politely pulled the chair out for her.

"*You* have the omelet," Andra said between clenched teeth.

"No, I'll eat the *frittata*," Drew offered generously, "you have the . . ."

"*I'll* eat the *fri*—the damn scrambled eggs," she practically screamed, plopping herself down in the chair in front of it.

Without another word, Drew sat down next to Andra.

In the tense silence that followed, Drew took several leisurely sips of his Bloody Mary while his mind worked frantically trying to find a way to save his hand. Like an opponent who'd gotten lucky, drawing an inside straight against eleven to one odds, Andra's unexpected play for the divorce papers this early in the game had forced a shift in his strategy. It was a good thing he'd covered himself by talking Mel into taking that vacation he'd been promising Norma and the kids for ages.

Waiting for her stomach to settle down before inflicting the *"frittata"* on it, Andra took several desperate sips of her Bloody Mary. Drew was obviously planning on making things as difficult as possible, she thought miserably. Her intuition had been correct: he meant to get back at her for leaving him the way she had, hurting his pride.

"Mmm, delicious," Drew mumbled around a mouthful of omelet in an attempt to get things back to where they were between them before the question of the divorce papers had come up. Indicating Andra's plate with his fork, he added solicitously, "Don't you think you should eat that before it gets cold?"

Anything she did to those eggs now could only be an improvement, she thought wryly as she took another swallow of her drink. Grudgingly, she had to admit that Drew still made the best Bloody Mary she'd ever tasted.

"Andra, why are you so upset?" Drew drawled soothingly while buttering a toasted bagel. "Instead of leaving Monday morning, you can leave Monday evening. It's only a few hours difference."

"I'm not upset, I'm angry," she managed to say coolly, reaching for her fork. Her hand was trembling. She *was* upset. The thought of spending another day with Drew unnerved her. They'd been together less than an hour that morning and she was already a nervous wreck. She didn't know how she was going to get through the next two days . . . three days now!

No matter how hard she tried to shut out the memories of the countless brunches she and Drew had shared in this very room, she couldn't. Everything conspired against her. The desert sunlight, flat and sharp as a knife, still sliced through the ceiling-to-floor windows, turning the tawny sandstone walls golden yellow. She'd always loved the way it bounced off the sandstone portions of the walls, highlighting the layers of colors buried within, how it brought out the warm reddish tone of the contemporary maple furniture and the thin beams that trimmed the cathedral ceiling.

The changing rays of the sun during the course of the day, which constantly altered the colors of the room, were echoed by the impressionistic yellow, orange, and red stripes of the huge rug that was the first purchase she and Drew had made for the house. Every objet d'art they'd collected, every souvenir from their travels, every fun gift they'd given one another was in its place, a physical reminder of their life together.

But the most disturbing physical reminder of all was Drew. His every movement and expression, the tone of his voice, even his silences, stirred suppressed feelings deep inside her, filling her with an old, familiar longing.

"Besides, I thought you agreed to help me," Drew went on, shattering her thoughts while he offered her half of the buttered bagel. "I really need your help."

"*My* help?" Andra muttered suspiciously, but she

accepted the bagel. "You mean you didn't just make that up?"

"Why would I make that up?" His eyes widened with hurt surprise. "Andra, haven't I always been honest with you?"

"Yes," she admitted grudgingly as she started pushing her food around on her plate. "But I'm on the other side of the table now," she tossed his words from last night back at him. It bothered her that they still hurt.

Drew suppressed a wry smile. He couldn't help admiring Andra's quick intelligence any more than he could help acknowledging an opponent's perfectly executed bluff even when he was beaten by it. He felt an old familiar tension beginning to coil inside him, a widening hunger. He devoured another mouthful of omelet.

Andra had to smile when she saw how lustily Drew attacked his food.

"This really is delicious," he said with a sexy little groan like a man who'd been starved for homemade omelets. He ran the tip of his tongue over his lips, savoring the taste that clung moistly to them. Andra's breath got stuck in her throat, and her own lips parted unconsciously.

Drew smiled. His darkening gaze caught and held hers for a long moment before sliding down to her mouth, where it lingered with an even greater hunger. "I've really missed this." The huskiness in his tone made it clear that he wasn't talking about the omelet.

"The suspense is killing me," Andra got out dryly after she'd managed to get the food down her suddenly constricted throat. Mercifully, the scrambled egg mess tasted better than it looked. "Just how can I help you?"

"I'm planning to write a book about gambling," he told her between bites, his voice and eyes neutral once more. "Not on how to gamble, but on how to expose the gaffs cardsharps use to rip off unsuspecting players."

"How can I help you with that?"

"The way I see it, the book will be primarily photographs. I'm still not sure how to go about it. . . ." He paused to take a thoughtful sip of his Bloody Mary. "I'd like to find some way to show my hands in the actual process of bottom dealing, say, or stacking a deck."

"You mean you want to show how it's done, step by step?" Unconsciously, she leaned across the table toward him as he nodded in agreement. "Well, you could do close-ups of your hands," she offered, her eyes following the sure, elegant movements of Drew's talented hands as he continued eating. She forced herself not to remember just how talented they were. "Uuh, a series of close-ups, shot by shot as they're stacking the deck."

"Yes, that's it," he said excitedly. "Would it work?"

"I think it's a terrific idea," Andra said sincerely. She was relieved to know that Drew wasn't trying to put something over on her as she'd feared.

"Well, it was your idea."

"My idea?"

"Sure. You told me once that I should write a book about my gambling experiences." A mocking smile lifted the corners of his moustache, giving him a devilish look. "Don't you remember—when you were still trying to reform me?" He paused to enjoy her discomfort. "Using captioned photos was my idea. So you think it would work?"

"I don't believe it's ever been done," she said, going back to her food. "I'm sure there must be a market for it."

"The publisher I've already talked to seemed to think so." Using a chunk of his bagel, Drew slid the remaining piece of omelet onto his fork. "He assured me that if I got a couple of sample chapters together, and he liked what he saw, he'd buy it."

"That's great, Drew," Andra blurted out with more enthusiasm than she would have liked to show.

"He's a lousy gambler but a very good publisher." Drew laughed warmly. Andra realized that it was the first time that weekend that Drew's laughter didn't have a wry or bitter edge to it. "Will you do it?" The look he gave her was also warm and open, with an uncharacteristic trace of pleading. It snagged something deep inside her. "Will you work with me?"

For one mindless moment, Andra was tempted by Drew's proposal; then she reminded herself of why she was there and what was sure to happen if she spent any length of time with him. She started fiddling with the remaining food on her plate. "You don't need me, Drew. There are plenty of photographers who would jump at the idea."

"But you're the only one I can trust, Andra. In spite of everything, you're still the only person I know that I trust implicitly," he allowed flatly before he finished his Bloody Mary. "I don't have to tell you how paranoid I am about my work. I'm not about to divulge secrets it's taken me a lifetime to acquire to anybody else."

"I'm sorry, Drew." Andra shifted uncomfortably in her seat. "Under the circumstances, I don't see how we can work together."

"Circumstances?" He looked at her blankly for a moment. "Oh, you mean the divorce?" An ironic smile flickered across his face. "But I thought you were the one who intended it to be a friendly divorce."

Not as friendly as you're intending it, Andra thought wryly as she went back to concentrating on her food. "It just wouldn't work out, Drew. A project like this would take months, and I'm leaving on . . ."

"All we need is a couple of chapters to begin with," he interrupted, leaning toward her.

"Even that would take weeks, and I'm flying back to New York Monday morning—evening."

"Do you really have to go?" he asked casually. "As a free-lance photographer, you've always made your own time." He moved closer and she caught a whiff of her favorite aftershave lotion and the smoky tang of his breath. "Is there some other job you're working on at the moment?"

Confused by his closeness and her own mixed-up feelings, Andra blurted out, "No, I'd finished up everything before I left, but . . ." The look that flashed in Drew's eyes stopped her cold. He already knew that, she realized; he knew her so well, he'd counted on it!

Drew was quick to drop his eyes, but Andra had seen that look too many times not to recognize it: pure triumph. That was how Drew always looked after scoring a big win. He *was* trying to trick her—but why?

Pushing away from the table, Andra got to her feet

angrily. "Are you planning on putting this gaff in the book too?"

"What gaff?" Drew sat back in his chair, making himself look up at Andra with utter astonishment. Mentally, he kicked himself for letting his real feelings show. Why was it so difficult for him to keep a poker face with her? And he'd almost had her! Reminding himself that he still had his ace in the hole made it easier to force a perplexed frown. "What are you talking about?"

"Oh, what's the use! I wouldn't believe anything you said now anyway." Sighing with angry frustration, she shifted from one foot to the other. "Will you at least answer one question honestly?"

"Sure, as many questions as you like."

"If I don't work with you, will you still give me a no-fault divorce, or are you planning on fighting it out in court now?"

"Of course you can have your goddamn no-fault divorce!" Sudden, uncontrollable anger brought Drew to his feet in one powerful motion. He knew that he was rapidly losing control of the game and fought to retain it. "I'm not trying to blackmail you."

"Then what *are* you trying to do? So far you've done everything possible to make things as difficult as you could," she said accusingly. "And you swore you wouldn't. That's why I agreed to come to Vegas. I didn't even have to be here."

"You would have liked that, wouldn't you, Andra?" he drawled sarcastically, but barely controlled anger still tautened every muscle of his powerful body. "Having everything taken care of for you. Nice and easy. No fuss. No messy emotional scenes."

"That's not true," she cried, stung that he would think that of her. "I just don't see why we should hurt each other any more than we already have."

"I've never deliberately hurt you . . . never!" The game had turned real, was completely out of Drew's control now, and there was nothing he could do about it. "*I'm* the one who came home one night and found a note on the bed we'd made love in only hours before telling me you'd left me!" He moved in on her and she stepped back. She'd never seen him so out of control. "Didn't you know that would rip me up? Or is that why you did it?"

"Did you ever think of how *I* felt when you got out of that bed and put your clothes back on and went out to play a poker game?" she lashed back with all the hurt and anger she hadn't realized had been festering inside her for almost a year. "You knew how upset I was. We'd gone to Paul's funeral only that morning— and all I could see was *you* lying in that coffin!" She fought to hold back the tears pushing behind her eyes and tying her vocal cords into knots. "Drew, I told you I couldn't go on living like that anymore."

He muttered a raw curse, but it was meant for himself, not for her; then all the anger went out of him. "You're right." He stared down at a spot on the floor. "I acted like an arrogant, insensitive idiot. But I'd thought that after we'd made love . . . the way we'd made love . . ."

He sighed harshly. "I was wrong." The pain was twisting inside him as it had that night; it was all over his face when he looked up at her again. "But you didn't have to walk out on me like that, Andra, leaving me nothing. Just that goddamn note." He moved in on her again, but there was no angry threat behind his action this time, only a weary sadness that hushed his tone. "Why couldn't you have waited for me to come home? We could have talked it out."

"But we wouldn't have talked it out, Drew," Andra reminded him ruefully. "We would have ended up the way we always did when I tried to tell you how unhappy I was about the way we were living. You would have made love to me, and I would have given in to you." Even now she had to fight the impulse to reach out and touch him, to wipe away the pain that lingered deep in his eyes, hurting her. "That's why I left the note. Because I knew that if I saw you again, if you so much as touched me, I'd never be able to . . ." She stopped herself just in time. She'd already said too much.

"Then you still cared for me?" he asked intensely. He moved closer, so close she could see the tiny vein beating in his jaw, feel the heat emanating from his body. "And you still care for me now, don't you?"

"What's the use of dragging up the past?" she said evasively, turning away so he wouldn't see the tears forcing their way into her eyes. She didn't know how long she could hold them back. Stepping quickly over to the table, she started collecting the dishes. "It's too late now. Can't we just end it without causing each other any more pain?"

"You didn't answer my question, Andra," Drew said tightly, coming to her side. "Do you still . . . will you leave those damn dishes alone?" Grabbing her wrist, he spun her around to face him. The plate slid out of her hand, spilling the scrambled egg mess all over the table.

It seemed to Andra that her life was as big a mess, and it infuriated her. "Drew, it's over . . . finished!" She pulled away from him so violently she staggered back several steps. "We've got to make a new life for ourselves."

"I'm glad it's so easy for you," he ground out bitterly.

"No, it's not easy for me. Stop saying that!" Andra finally exploded. "None of it has been easy—leaving you, or this past year, or going through this now!" Tears filling her eyes, she turned to make for the door, but Drew grabbed her arm, holding her back.

"You still care for me, damn it! Why won't you admit it?" His other hand grabbed her free arm, and he pulled her against him. "And it's not over between us, not by a long shot," he grated almost angrily before his mouth came down hard on hers.

Her startled cry was muffled by the bruising, burning crush of his mouth. One hand shot around her back to mold her body to the strong, taut length of his; the other tangled deep in her hair to keep her from twisting her head free. Hunger battled anger and frustration in his kiss. Hunger won.

The way Drew was holding her, Andra was powerless to move, defenseless against the rush of echoing hunger that went ripping through her. She might have been able to resist his superior strength, but not the intensity of the desire that coiled his powerful muscles, the uncontrollable tremor that shook his strength. She'd never been able to resist that.

She still wanted him, she realized desperately, had never stopped wanting him. She could feel the barriers she'd so carefully erected against him the past year begin to disintegrate, everything in her beginning to open to him. She couldn't believe that he could still do this to her.

She pressed her hands against his shoulders to push him away, but the familiar feel of his muscles, the way they still curved into her palms and contracted at her touch, made her grab onto them instead. Drew groaned as he felt her fingers dig into him and his kiss deepened, became devouring, as he tightened his hold on her. She could feel the warmth of his body right through to her bones, could feel her own body heating under it. It's not fair, she thought dazedly as her mouth opened under the consuming pressure of his; it's just not fair.

His tongue thrust deep inside her with that old possessiveness, deep hard thrusts that left her clinging to him with every part of her. Suddenly, his hand tightened in her hair, pulling her head back so he could see deep into her eyes. "Now tell me it's over between us," he ground out. "Tell me how you don't care for me anymore."

Andra's thick lashes fluttered down to hide the naked truth in her eyes, to block out the love and desire burning in his. "It doesn't matter how I feel about you," she got out miserably, "because nothing has changed."

"*Everything's* changed," he rasped before his mouth took hers again, "except the way we feel about each other."

7

Drew's mouth moved softly on Andra's this time, sensuously, and his fingers released her hair to slide down her back. He hasn't forgotten anything, she thought helplessly, as his tongue explored her mouth deeply, with a knowing intimacy. His hands moved expertly over her body, lingering erotically on her most sensitive areas.

Andra's body remembered also, responding to Drew's every touch as completely as it used to, softening, melting into him. Her delicate arms went up to wrap themselves tightly around his neck. Mindlessly, she returned his kiss with all the love and passion he'd always evoked in her.

"Christ, Andra, I'm crazy about you," Drew rasped when he dragged his mouth away. "I've always been crazy about you. How could you have ever doubted it?" His arms tightened around her until she could barely breathe. "Tell me you still want me," he insisted fiercely, as if he needed to hear her say what was already obvious to both of them. "Tell me!"

"Yes." She sighed breathlessly. "I do. I want you . . . so much."

With a deep groan of satisfaction, Drew slid both arms down Andra's back. Bending swiftly, he scooped her up effortlessly in his arms, taking the weight of her slender body against his strong chest. He hesitated for a moment, expecting her to protest. When she didn't —couldn't—he spun around with sudden urgency to carry her up to the bedroom, his carefully worked-out game plan in shreds.

Andra's arms gripped Drew's neck as he carried her upstairs. She felt herself falling, still held in his sure, hard embrace, but falling irrevocably away from herself. In a few moments, she recalled, she would be completely lost in him. "Oh, I knew I shouldn't have come here," she murmured futilely. "I knew this would happen." Burying her face in his neck, she burst into tears.

She felt his sharp, surprised intake of breath against her body just as he was about to carry her over the threshold into the bedroom. "Don't, love . . . please don't," he pleaded in her hair. "It's okay." He came to a halt and the powerful muscles in his arms—taut with sexual tension—softened, became a warm cradle around her. "Everything's going to be okay now."

Drew wanted nothing more than to carry Andra over the threshold into the bedroom, to prove to her how much he loved her, how good it was going to be with them again. But her very defenselessness made it impossible for him to go on making love to her. He knew that she wouldn't stop him, but she might misinterpret his motives afterward and assume that he just wanted her sexually, and then she would hate him. He wasn't about to make that mistake again.

With a heavy sigh, Drew turned and carried Andra back downstairs to the living room. He crooned soothing words in her fragrant hair, a muffled lullaby, as he moved down the carpeted steps of the conversation pit. Carrying her to the custom-made sofa, which encircled a free-standing fireplace, he set her gently down on the thick cushions. He remained standing in front of her.

Drew longed to hold Andra in his arms and comfort her, but he was sure that would only upset her more and make it difficult for him to get himself back under control—back to his game plan. Seducing her was not part of his carefully worked-out strategy. He didn't intend just to get her into bed; he wanted his wife back. But when she'd told him that it was over between them, had flung it in his face with such certainty, he'd lost all control.

Watching her now, her tears threatening his control again, Drew warned himself against letting his emotions get the better of him. "Are you all right now?" he asked, his tone neutral. "Can I get you anything? A brandy?"

Without looking up at him, Andra shook her head and took a couple of long, deep breaths. Instead of helping her to recover, they released more of the tears that had been frozen inside her for the past year. "Oh, what's the matter with me?" she wailed, brushing the tears away with both hands. "How could I have let this happen?"

"It's okay, love," Drew murmured reassuringly. "Everything's going to be okay now, I promise."

Andra laughed unexpectedly, a short, ironic laugh that sounded more like a sob, and fresh tears streamed down her face.

It tore at Drew, and he had to fight to remain in the game. It was a game he couldn't afford to lose, he reminded himself. Instinctively, he knew that now was the time to spring his ace in the hole, while she was still vulnerable, before she could recover sufficiently to put up that defensive wall between them again.

"Andra, listen to me," he said sharply, sitting down beside her but at a nonthreatening distance. "What if I told you that I'd give up being a professional gambler, the way you always wanted me to? Would you give our marriage another chance?"

She looked up at him with misty silver eyes, lashes sparkling with tears. Her face was still flushed, and her soft lips trembled as they parted in surprise. Desire surged in Drew again, hot and hard. He wanted her so badly, he ached. His hands clenched around the bottom edge of the sofa cushions to keep from grabbing her.

"You . . . give up gambling?" she breathed incredulously. A flicker of hope lit up her eyes but was quickly extinguished. "Oh, you were always promising to give up gambling," she reminded herself with a rueful smile. "Someday."

"Someday is here, love," Drew stated firmly. He paused, as he always did just before he turned over the winning hand. "I haven't been a professional gambler for over a month."

"What?" She blinked uncomprehendingly. A last

tear clung to her bottom lashes, and it slipped down her cheek without her noticing. "What would you call what you were doing last night?"

"It's called being a gambling investigator." He grinned broadly. "My first legitimate job."

Drew looked so proud of himself, Andra had to believe him. "What's a gambling investigator? I mean, what do you do?"

"My job is to expose crooked gamblers. Over the years, I've just about learned every trick in the book in order to protect myself. So when the owner of a casino or private gambling club suspects that there's a mechanic working the tables, I'm hired to spot him." Leaning comfortably back against the back of the sofa, Drew crossed his long legs. He looked very pleased with himself. "They pay me a considerable fee and cover my losses," he went on confidently. "And since the money I win doesn't come out of their till, I get to keep that too, except for their usual cut, of course."

Andra sat there quietly, as if she needed a moment to grasp fully the implications of Drew's words. Having already experienced her enthusiastic response in his mind a few hundred times, Drew found himself actually savoring the pause before it finally hit her.

"Oh, my God," she cried, appalled, and jumped up from the couch. "But that's even worse than what you were doing before! Why on earth did you do that?" She waited for his answer, for some explanation to what she clearly considered to be madness.

For a moment, Drew was too stunned to respond. He felt like a man holding four aces who'd just been beaten out by a royal flush. "What do you mean?"

"You're putting yourself in more danger than ever,"

she protested. "What happens when one of those crooks finds out that you put the finger on him?"

"Andra, I'm not in any real danger," Drew said with a dismissive wave of his hand. "I'm dealing with cardsharps, not hit men. They're petty criminals." He shrugged lightly. "Cheating is their game, not violence."

"What about that man last night? He looked pretty violent to me," she said, challenging him. "Is he a cardsharp?"

"Yeah, I'm pretty sure he's the one who slipped a cooler—a marked deck—into the game. But I have to prove it."

"He was about to attack you just because you won. What if he—"

"But he didn't attack me, Andra," Drew said, cutting her off. Impatience crept into his tone, bringing him to his feet in one lithe motion. "And I took care of him without having to use force. You saw that."

"But when you expose him and he finds out," she persisted anxiously, "what happens then?"

"He'll just slink back into whatever hole he crawled out of. He sure in hell won't be able to show his face in this town anymore."

"But how can you be sure?" she cried, fear widening her eyes and constricting her voice.

Drew ground out an exasperated curse under his breath and turned away from Andra. This was not how the game was supposed to play, he thought wretchedly, reaching into his shirt pocket for his cigarette case. Like a badly stacked deck, all the cards were falling the wrong way. He took his time lighting up, shuffling through the arguments he'd prepared so carefully in his mind and searching for the one that would win Andra over.

"You're exaggerating the danger, love. You always did," he said soothingly when he turned back to her. "The important thing to remember is that I won't be out gambling practically every night with my own money—*our* money." He moved closer, just enough to force her to be aware of him but not enough to alarm her. "You remember how it used to be? I'd be riding high one week, down in the cellar the next. Remember?"

The memory flickered over Andra's face, clouding her eyes. She nodded affirmatively.

"And I'm sure that bad-luck streak I was on the last couple of months we were together had a lot to do with the trouble we were having, and . . ." He paused to take a long, hard drag on his cigarette. The smoke came out in a hard rush. ". . . and why you left me, but now—"

"Drew, it wasn't the money," Andra interjected sharply. "It was your life-style that I couldn't live with or the kind of people you were associating with. I was always afraid you'd get . . . hurt. And then when Paul was murdered . . . that horrible way . . ." She still couldn't talk about it without experiencing a paralyzing knot of fear in the pit of her stomach. She was stunned to find that the thought of something similar happening to Drew could still devastate her.

"Andra," Drew said as he exhaled impatiently on a long stream of smoke, "the kind of trouble Paul got himself into had nothing to do with gambling. Why do you still refuse to believe that?"

"Because I still can't forget it," she cried angrily. "And I'm afraid the same thing could happen to you!"

"But it wouldn't happen to me," he insisted. "Paul tried to pull off a crooked deal, and he was dumb enough to try it with the wrong people. I'd never get involved in such a setup."

"But the setup you're involved in now is almost as dangerous."

"That's not true," he objected, the force of his need to make her believe him bringing him closer. "Everything's going to be okay now, you'll see."

Andra stepped back to get away from the disturbing closness of his body, the even more disturbing appeal in his eyes that threatened her resolve. "Drew, nothing's really changed. Can't you see that?"

"Everything's changed!"

"Well, one thing certainly hasn't," Andra countered with a hopeless sigh. "I can't get you to understand why I feel this way . . . and you can't get me to see it your way."

"Obviously," Drew muttered before taking one last pull on his cigarette. Stepping over to the cocktail table, he squashed the butt out in the ashtray. The filter tip broke off under the harsh pressure of his hand, scattering brown bits of tobacco. "And I'd thought this was what you wanted." A bitter smile twisted the corners of his mouth as he sank heavily back down on the sofa. "You'd always said it was what you wanted."

"Drew, what I wanted was for us to have a normal life . . . a family," Andra explained on her way over to him. She was about to sit down next to him but decided not to—her feelings had a way of betraying her every time she got too close to him. She would need every bit of reasoning power she possessed if she was ever going to get through to him. "And we could never have a normal life unless you got out of gambling for good."

"That's why I took this job, Andra," Drew pointed out flatly. "This job is the first step. The book is another." Shaking his head in frustration, he hunched over, resting his forearms on his knees. He stared down at the floor as if he couldn't bring himself to look at her. "I'm thirty-seven years old. I barely finished high school. Everything I know I've taught myself. What kind of job do you think I could get?"

He looked up at her then, and Andra was stunned by the expression on his face—he looked lost, hopelessly lost. She'd never seen him like that and it tugged at something inside her. She had to stop herself from going to him.

"You're the one who has all the answers," he added dryly. "You tell me."

"Drew, I . . ." Andra shifted from one foot to the other, torn between love and fear, between longing to help him and trying to save herself. "I don't know," she admitted lamely.

"Well, I sure in hell don't," Drew said, his voice grim. He dug into his shirt pocket for his cigarette case again. He'd never felt so totally defeated in his life. He knew that he should be planning a fresh strategy, but he was no longer able to play the game. All he could do was put his cards on the table—and hope that she didn't wipe him out.

"I love you, Andra," he said tightly, staring down at

the gold case gleaming in his hands. "I've never stopped loving you . . . but it wasn't for lack of trying." A wry smile quirked his mouth as he flicked open the cigarette case. "I did everything I could to get you out of my system. Nothing worked." Unconsciously, he rubbed his thumb over the loving words Andra had had inscribed inside the case as though he were reading them like braille. "I guess I never realized how much a part of me you were until I lost you." Sliding a cigarette out abruptly, he snapped the case shut.

Andra started involuntarily. It seemed to her that the metal click was as loud as a gunshot in the aching silence that hung between them. She hadn't realized that she'd stopped breathing.

"I want you back," Drew went on, fumbling the lighter out of his pocket. He had to flick it several times before he got it to light. Taking a slow, deep pull on his cigarette, he let the smoke out in ragged pieces. "That's the real reason—the *only* reason I insisted that you come back to Vegas."

With a soundless gasp, Andra sank down onto the sofa next to Drew.

From his hunched-over position, he sent her a searching look to see what effect his words were having before he risked making an even bigger fool of himself.

She seemed barely able to deal with the intense emotion suffusing her sensitive face. Her eyes were misty with tears again, intensifying the soft, warm glow in their silvery depths, which he'd never been able to forget, had feared he'd never see again. It was more than Drew had hoped for, and he had to stop himself from reaching over and grabbing her. But it gave him the encouragement to go on, a fresh determination to win her back at any cost.

"And that's the only reason I took on this job and the book, why I set it up so you'd have to stay here at the house with me," Drew continued, his voice husky with the longing he could no longer conceal. "I was hoping that if you remembered all the good things we had together, I could get you to love me again."

"Oh, Drew, but I . . ." Andra had to bite down on her bottom lip to keep from blurting out her real feelings. This was how he'd always managed to get around her, she warned herself, by playing on her love for him. If she admitted how much she still loved him—more than she'd dared to admit to herself until then—she'd be completely at his mercy.

Realizing instantly that Andra was withdrawing from him again, Drew dropped his cigarette into the ashtray and shifted his body around completely, managing to slide closer to her as he did. "Could you still love me, Andra?"

"Drew, love isn't enough," she got out evasively, struggling to defend herself against the naked pleading in his voice and eyes that was pulling at her, drawing her irrevocably away from herself, toward him. "Love wasn't enough the first time."

"Running away from it didn't work either, did it?" he said bluntly. His arm shot out in front of her breasts, taut fingers locking onto the top of the cushion behind her shoulder. It amazed her that he knew she was about to get up almost before she did. "You can run away again," he taunted, moving closer, blocking off any chance of escape with his powerful body. "You

110

can refuse to deal with the love you know we both feel for each other, but you can't destroy it."

"The way we were living *was* destroying it," Andra said in a strained voice, pulling back against the seat cushions. "All the arguments we were having . . . that's why I had to go away. We would have ended up hating each other." Her voice broke from the pain that thought still caused her. "And that's what will happen if we—"

"No! Everything's going to be different now, you'll see," Drew insisted fiercely. "There was never anything wrong between us, love. The only problems we had were external ones. We can work them out." His hands moved so quickly to grip her shoulders they were a blur. Bending his head, he brought his face down to hers. "Andra, isn't that the real reason you came back to Vegas?"

Andra froze. That couldn't have been the reason— could it? "No," she protested defensively. "I came here only to get the divorce."

"There isn't going to be any divorce!" His voice was savage but his eyes held more pain then anger. Suddenly demanding fingers dug into her flesh, pulling her away from the back of the sofa. Her breasts brushed his chest and the breath caught in her throat, making it impossible for her to protest. He sucked in a sharp breath at the feel of her but didn't move. His eyes darkened and his lips parted sensuously, hungrily.

Andra knew that Drew was about to kiss her and that she wouldn't be able to stop him. She felt her heartbeat quicken in anticipation and realized that she wanted him to kiss her, that she wanted nothing more than to forget their insoluble problems in his warm, vibrant arms—to forget everything.

Only the discipline a lifetime of gambling had taught Drew kept him from kissing Andra, and the fear that in overplaying his hand he would lose her for good. The effort it cost him made his hands shake. "We can work it out, love," he insisted softly. "I'll do everything I can." His hands released her shoulders to glide down her arms, but his mouth remained a breath away and his every word was a caress. "Please . . . just meet me halfway. That's all I ask."

"But . . . how?"

"Don't go back to New York on Monday." His hands found and caught hers, creating a circle of warmth in her lap. "Stay and work with me on the book for a couple of weeks and we'll see how—"

"You mean, stay here at the house with you . . . like before?"

"Yes. But not as man and wife," Drew was quick to amend when he felt her hands tense in his. "Not until . . . unless you agree to give our marriage another chance."

"Drew, you know what will happen if we're together all the time." Andra fell back against the seat cushions with a hopeless sigh. "You saw what almost happened earlier."

"It won't happen again, I swear." As if to prove that he meant what he'd said, he straightened, letting go of her hands. "You've always accused me of using sex to solve our problems—and you were right," he admitted openly. "I'll never do that to you again."

Andra was completely thrown by Drew's admission

and his obvious determination to change. Yet every rugged line of his face, every vibrant muscle in his body still radiated pure sexuality. She had to look away. "I wish I could believe you."

Hard fingers closed on her chin, pulling her face back to his. "Andra, I could have been making love to you right this minute," he reminded her bluntly. "You weren't about to stop me." Midnight eyes, burning with the memory, locked with hers, and she was unable to break their hold—or deny the truth. "I stopped it. And I meant what I said last night," he added, his voice raw. "I can't . . . I won't make love to you knowing that there's even a chance that I'll find another note on the bed afterward."

Andra flinched as if he had slapped her.

Drew's thumb slowly traced the line of her jaw, and his voice softened with regret. "I'm not trying to get you back in my bed, love. I want you back in my life . . . for good."

Releasing her abruptly, Drew reached for his cigarette. It had been burning down in the ashtray and there was barely a puff left, but he took it. His hand was unsteady. It occurred to him that he'd faced showdowns in championships games, covering bets of $50,000 or more without turning a hair, and here he was dying inside while he waited for Andra to make her move.

With a sigh, she shifted in her seat and looked up at him. "All right, Drew," she said softly, a bit fearfully. "I'll meet you halfway."

8

〜∞∞∞∞∞∞∞∞〜

Did I remember to get everything?" asked Drew politely. Standing in the doorway, he watched as Andra completed a brisk, efficient tour of the fully equipped darkroom he'd had set up for her the first year they were married. "If I've forgotten anything, we can pick it up in Vegas later."

Crossing in front of the enlarger, Andra started over to him with a sarcastic smile. "You've thought of absolutely everything." Her tone made it clear that she wasn't just referring to the bright yellow boxes of film, the bottles of developing fluid, or the reams of photography paper stacked neatly alongside the processing trays.

What the hell did she mean by that? Drew wondered. Why was she on the defensive again? They'd been getting along so well. After cleaning up the kitchen, they'd spent the rest of the afternoon brainstorming a format for the book. She'd seemed to be as excited about it as he was, and he'd expected her to be pleased to find the darkroom ready for her.

"What's wrong?" With a perplexed frown, Drew backed out of the doorway to let Andra by. "I was just trying to make things as easy as possible."

Easy, Andra thought, fuming. That's what she'd always been where he was concerned—easy—and he'd counted on that. She slammed the door shut behind her, making the dart board attached to it bang against the wood.

The rest of the paneled basement was a game room. A seven-sided poker table stood in the center like an altar, its baize top protected by a dust cover. Over it dangled a large, green-shaded light. A pair of identical light fixtures were suspended over the shrouded pool table that took up the length of one wall. Against the other wall was an old-fashioned ice cream parlor counter that served as a bar. In a corner, next to a couple of lounge chairs, was a vintage 1940's jukebox filled with Billie Holiday records.

Impulsively, Andra picked up a handful of darts and paced off the required distance. She set herself and aimed. "You were pretty sure of yourself, weren't you?" The dart flew out of her hand. It sliced into the very center of the bull's-eye, red tail feathers quivering from the impact.

A slow smile curved Drew's mouth. He had the distinct feeling that Andra would have preferred using him as a dart board.

"I'm never sure of myself where you're concerned,

love," he admitted wryly. A dart whizzed past him as he made his way over to her. "That's why I have to do anything and everything I can to better my odds."

Her response was another quick, hard throw, but the dart landed in the circle below the bull's-eye this time.

"Andra, I didn't go ahead and buy the photography equipment because I was sure of myself," Drew persisted, coming to her side. "I just wanted to prove to you that I was serious about our working on the book together." She continued ignoring him to focus on her aim. "You can't blame me for doing everything I can to get you back."

Her hand jerked just as she was releasing the dart. It missed the board completely and went zinging into the door. She shot him a look as sharp as any of the darts before stalking over to the cork board.

"Would you like to play a game?" offered Drew lightly, attempting to put Andra in a responsive mood again.

"Play a game with *you*?" She laughed sardonically and began tugging the darts out of the board. "No way."

"Why not?"

Her hand hesitated on the dart that was stuck in the door. "Because I can never win with you." Once again, her tone implied more than her words.

"Yes, you can," Drew returned in kind. She threw him a guarded look over her shoulder. "Come on, love," he urged, his voice light again, almost boyishly eager. "I'll play you with one hand behind my back."

She turned to face him and reminded him wryly,

"Darts are supposed to be played with only one hand."

"Then I'll play you with just my thumb and"—he stuck his index finger straight up in the air—"one finger."

Andra laughed in spite of herself. "You can do more with one finger than most men can do with both hands . . . oh." She was made embarrassingly aware of her double entendre by the grin spreading across his face, the wicked gleam in his eyes.

"And I didn't think you remembered," he drawled provocatively.

She turned away from him, from the evocative pull of shared memories, and tossed the darts into the wooden holder. "That's enough of *that* game," she muttered pointedly. "Time to get back to work." Sweeping past him, she made resolutely for the stairs.

"I think we've done enough work for one day," said Drew, following Andra upstairs. He tried to keep his eyes off the feminine, sensuous sway of her hips, but he couldn't. It was all he could do to keep his hands off her.

"I didn't realize how exhausting legitimate work could be," he went on, trying to joke, to keep the memory of how her softly rounded hips felt under his hands from taking over his mind completely. "I really don't think I should overdo it the first day."

"Well, I wouldn't want you to strain anything," Andra teased, then swore silently. Why did everything she said have a double meaning to it? she wondered, pushing through the door leading to the first-floor landing. As long as they were working, she had no trouble dealing with him. What was she going to do now?

"Besides, it's time we dressed for dinner," Drew added, stopping beside her. "The tournament isn't until nine, so . . ."

"You mean you still intend to go to the game," she interrupted anxiously, "and expose that horrible man?"

"It's my job, Andra," he reminded her quietly. "You agreed to meet me halfway." He looked down into her wide, troubled eyes. "Will you come with me?"

She nodded reluctantly.

He sighed with relief. "Let's make a big night of it, okay? We'll have a great dinner and take in a show."

"But I didn't bring the right clothes," she cut in. "All I packed were casual things and a business suit."

One bushy black eyebrow went up. "A business suit, for Vegas?"

"For the lawyer's."

"You won't be needing *that*," he promised darkly; then, as if he'd suddenly remembered something, he brightened again. "Come with me, love," he said cheerfully, grabbing her hand. "I know how we can fix you up."

"What do you mean?" Andra asked as she found herself being helped up the stairs to the second floor.

"You'll see," Drew said.

That was all he would say until they were standing in front of the large walk-in closet in the master bedroom. Sliding the doors open, he indicated the row of evening gowns that still hung in her half of the closet. A wry smile lifted the corners of his moustache. "You forgot to pack these when you left."

As he obviously realized, Andra hadn't forgotten to pack them. She'd deliberately left them behind with the life-style that went with them.

"Styles can't have changed that much in less than a year," Drew went on. "Your measurements certainly haven't." His gaze moved over every curve of her body with intimate knowledge. "You should be able to put together an outfit for this evening."

The sweep of his hand included the dressy shoes that were standing in a high-heeled row under the gowns and the glittering evening bags that were neatly lined up on the top shelf. "Let's see. . . ." His long, sensitive fingers glided from gown to gown with a soft, caressing motion. He smiled unconsciously, sensually, as if he were remembering how she looked in each and every one of the gowns.

His hand paused, lingering over the layered ruffles of the white chiffon gown she'd worn for their third-anniversary celebration. "I've always loved the way you look in this," he murmured, his voice thick with the memory of that love-filled night. The memory gleamed hot and bright in his eyes when they met hers. "Would you mind wearing this for me tonight?"

"All right," she said, swallowing quickly.

He flashed her one of those devastating smiles of his that always went right through her. "Thanks, love." Bending his head, he brushed her lips softly.

Before she could react, he walked out the door.

Saturday-night traffic was bumper to bumper along the Strip, which was ablaze with miles of soaring, multicolored neon signs. Twisted into fantastical shapes, spilling over the facades of gigantic hotel-casinos, the million-watt lights lit up the night sky, obliterating the stars. Sleek Porsches and Maseratis vied with pickup trucks, rental cars, and recreational vehicles—even a couple of motorcycles and a dune buggy—sporting license plates from all over the States.

The people jamming the sidewalks were just as eclectic an assortment: jean-clad to mink-clad, one-week-a-year gamblers to compulsive gamblers, care-free students on a spree to senior citizens betting their social security checks. They swarmed from casino to casino in search of the biggest jackpot, the hottest craps table, the luckiest spin of the wheel or turn of a card.

The excited buzz of the crowd played counterpoint to the blaring noise of the traffic, creating the perfect background music for the light show that was Vegas. A sci-fi touch was added by the futuristic Circus-Circus aerial tram, which shuttled guests between the hotel and the casino, where trapeze artists flew unnoticed over the patrons' heads as they gambled.

Andra laughed as she continued wending her way through the crowd with Drew. "I'd forgotten what an extraordinary place this is." She was feeling uncharacteristically generous toward Vegas that evening, prob-ably because she couldn't remember the last time she'd had so much fun.

She'd really enjoyed having dinner with Drew, once she got over her initial nervousness—more than she'd expected to. More than she should have. But then, she'd always enjoyed herself with him. Just as he was the only man who'd been able to evoke from her a depth of sexuality she never would have believed herself capable of, he alone was able to bring out the fun-loving, almost reckless side of her nature that her strict upbringing had taught her to suppress. They'd lingered, talking and laughing just like old times, over their after-dinner drinks for so long they ended up missing the show.

As if he could read her thoughts, or was sharing them, Drew sent Andra a warm smile. His strong, supple fingers, which were gripping her hand protectively, shifted, sliding between her fingers with an easy intimacy. Out of synch with the rest of the rushing, murmuring crowd, they continued their leisurely walk. They were both still caught up in the warm afterglow of the dinner they'd shared—a mellow kind of high that owed nothing to champagne or brandy.

"Here we are," Drew said reluctantly. He came to a halt in front of The Xanadu, Las Vegas's newest, gaudiest megahotel-casino. Its architectural style, all huge, glittering domes topped by gold spires, was Hollywood-Mongolian—enough to make Genghis Khan turn over in his mausoleum.

Somehow, that night, Andra appreciated the hotel's crazy kind of charm. She was feeling generous this evening!

"We've got almost an hour before the game," Drew told her, checking his watch. "What would you like to do?"

For a moment, Andra was too surprised to respond. Drew had always stubbornly refused to wear a watch, to allow time to dictate how he chose to spend it. It was a typical Las Vegas conceit: there wasn't a single clock to be found in any casino, nor were there any windows to help distinguish day from night and distract from the timeless unreality that pervaded the desert city.

"Part of my new image," explained Drew with a self-mocking smile when he saw Andra staring incredulously at his digital watch. "I told you I've changed, love." Promises glowed in his dark eyes as they held hers, and Andra found herself believing them. "So what would you like to do for the next . . ." he made a big show of checking his watch again . . . "fifty-three minutes and twenty-two seconds?"

"What else is there to do in Vegas except gamble?" She laughed for no reason—unless feeling unreasonably happy was a reason. "I feel lucky tonight."

"So do I," Drew murmured intensely, letting Andra know that he wasn't talking about gambling. He pulled open one of the glass entrance doors and held it for her.

Andra gasped as she came up against the wall of chilled air. With a photographer's eye, she was taking in the sights of the casino, the shifting pictures the milling crowd made, when Drew's hand closed around her arm abruptly and pulled her protectively to his side.

"Excuse us," he said politely to the huge gorilla of a man who'd just stepped into their path. The man studied Drew's face for a moment, then exchanged glances with an even scarier-looking man who was positioned at the opposite end of the wall of glass doors.

Andra was sure that they were part of the army of plainclothes guards hired to keep troublemakers and known cross-roaders out of the casino. But she felt a definite sense of relief when Drew pushed resolutely past the man, automatically shielding her with his body as he did.

"So where would you like to try your luck?" His hand relaxed on her arm, gliding down to clasp her hand lightly as they started down the aisle. "One-armed bandits?" He indicated the phalanx of slot machines standing at the ready to entice players the instant they stepped through the doors.

"That's how I got into trouble the first time," Andra teased, reminding Drew of the way they'd met.

She hadn't needed to remind him. "Luckiest night of my life," he murmured, his voice deep with feeling. Something turned over inside her.

A roar went up from one of the craps tables. "Sounds as if someone's on a roll." With a tug at her hand, Drew started toward the dice pit. "Want to get in on the action?"

Andra shook her head. The dice pit was the most frantic, raucous place in any casino. It was where gamblers looking for hard-core action went. Shooting craps was definitely out of her league. "Just a bit too much action for my taste."

"It's a game of pure chance." Drew shrugged his disinterest as they continued past the players chanting or shouting for their numbers to come up as the red dice flashed across the green baize. Groans mingled with whoops of triumph.

"So is roulette," Drew added with the same tone of condescension, making Andra smile. She knew that it was the challenge of the game that fascinated Drew, the consummate skill required to beat the odds and outmaneuver the sharpest minds in the business. Luck didn't interest him. He made his own luck.

"Besides, roulette has the worst odds of all," Andra said, deliberately imitating Drew's slightly superior tone. "They're outrageously stacked in favor of the house."

Drew shot Andra a look to see if she was putting him on; when he saw that she was, he grinned.

"You see," she said as they moved past the spinning wheel and the silver blur of the ball, "I still remember everything you taught me."

His grin widened. "Everything?"

"Now, in blackjack," Andra went on quickly, ignoring the wicked gleam in his eyes and her suddenly racing pulse, "the house has only a slight edge." She started down the steps leading to the blackjack pit ahead of him. "With strategy and shrewd betting, plus luck, a player has an almost even chance." She gave Drew a look over her shoulder. He was staring at something or someone in back of him. "Am I right, teacher?"

"Right," Drew agreed absently when he looked back at her. "Blackjack it is, then." He gave her a smile that didn't reach his eyes and waved her over to the double row of small horseshoe tables. Blue-backed cards flashed on either side as they moved between the tables, the luxurious carpet giving way beneath their feet. Unlike the raucous shouting in the dice pit and the muttered incantations at the roulette tables, an almost reverential hush pervaded the blackjack pit.

Since the two-dollar and five-dollar tables were all filled, Andra took a seat at one of the ten-dollar tables. Instead of taking the empty chair next to hers, Drew remained standing beside her. "Aren't you going to play?"

"Mr. R. isn't permitted to play, miss," the tall, gaunt dealer informed her in his clipped New England accent while briskly converting a losing player's one-hundred-dollar bill into chips.

"I don't understand," Andra murmured, amazed. She knew that Drew would never cheat; his pride wouldn't allow it. "Why not?" She spun around in her chair to face Drew, but his attention was fixed elsewhere again.

"Because he can count down the shoe," the dealer explained with a quick, possessive glance at the contraption he used to feed the cards out one by one. "Even though we use a triple deck." Folding the hundred-dollar bill neatly in half, he pushed it through the slot in the table into the locked box underneath. A smile of reluctant respect stretched his thin lips. "The way Mr. R. plays blackjack, it's no longer a game of chance."

Drew brought his attention back to the table. "I'm not playing." Reaching inside his dinner jacket, he unzipped the special money compartment. "The lady is playing. Unassisted."

"But I don't want to play without you," Andra protested. Sliding out of her chair, she made a quick apology to the other players, who were obviously impatient to get on with the game.

"The same thing's going to happen at baccarat," said Drew.

"Can you really count down the shoe . . . memorize three decks of cards?"

He nodded matter-of-factly as though it were the easiest thing in the world. "Looks as if it's going to have to be the slots. Sorry, love."

"I'm ashamed to admit it, but that's more my speed."

They had come full circle in their travels, and as they started over to the slot machines Drew cast a quick, furtive glance over his shoulder again. Curiosity finally got the better of Andra. Following the line of his gaze, she spotted the stunning-looking cocktail waitress who'd worked the Wild West saloon the night before. The curvaceous redhead was serving drinks at one of the blackjack tables where the gorillalike plainclothes guard was lounging about trying to look like a patron.

"I can't blame you for staring," Andra said tightly, her vocal cords in knots. "She's gorgeous."

"What?" Drew sounded genuinely perplexed. "Who?" Without slowing his steps, he looked over her shoulder again to see to whom she was referring. "You mean Sherry?" he asked as though he hadn't noticed the girl before. "Yeah . . ." He gave a dismissive shrug. "She's all right."

"All right?" Andra laughed. She'd meant the laugh to sound unconcerned and sophisticated; it came out anything but. "She could be a movie star, she's so . . . voluptuous."

A smile of pure masculine satisfaction played on Drew's lips when he realized that Andra—having jumped to the wrong conclusion—was jealous. He couldn't tell her the truth; he was still hoping that his suspicions would be proved wrong. He told himself that he was getting paranoid in his old age, but he would have felt better if the tiny hairs at the back of his neck, which always stood up when he sensed danger, would settle down. He quickened his step, trying not to be obvious about it, and forced a laugh. "Jealous?"

"Of course not," she lied proudly.

"You have no reason to be. Voluptuous doesn't turn me on," he said sincerely. Because of his work, he was constantly surrounded by beautiful young women who flaunted a sexuality he knew few of them possessed. "I prefer my women classy."

Drew's eyes swept over the soft, filmy layers of Andra's off-the-shoulder white chiffon gown, which swirled around her as she moved, emphasizing the delicate, exquisitely feminine curves of her body. The memory of her naked in his arms took him unawares and made his blood jump. "I prefer you," he admitted, his voice a husky murmur. "Always have."

Andra slid Drew a sardonic smile, but the matching comeback she'd prepared got stuck in her throat when she saw the naked longing in his eyes. For one suspended moment, the sights and sounds of the casino faded to nothing. They were the only two people in that vast crowded space, the emotion-charged electricity flowing between them the only reality. Then Drew tensed, as though he'd glimpsed something out of the corner of his eye, and broke the connection.

His hand tightened around her arm, pulling her close to his side. It was a protective rather than a sensual gesture, Andra noted dazedly, and his movements were guarded when he guided her down one of the many aisles between the slot machines. "Is everything all right, Drew?"

"Sure." He smiled reassuringly without meeting her

eyes and headed straight for the silver-dollar slots. "I say we go for broke. What do you say?"

"Broke is exactly what we'll be," she returned, trying to keep her tone as playful as his. Why couldn't she shake the feeling that something was wrong?

"Where's the change girl?" Using that as an excuse, Drew quickly scanned the area. The tiny hairs at the back of his neck stiffened. Damn, there he was again, he thought irritably.

Without appearing to, Drew watched the man in the next aisle who was making a show of feeding quarters into two machines at the same time. Again, Drew tried telling himself that he was getting paranoid, but he knew the odds too well. It had to be more than coincidence that everywhere they'd gone in the casino that big ape had been right on their heels. He'd sensed trouble when the man had first cut them off at the entrance. It was because of Andra, Drew realized, that he'd chosen to disregard his instincts.

It was Andra he was most concerned about now. Not for her safety, because he'd never allow any harm to come to her—just as he felt confident that he could take care of himself—but he didn't want anything to remind her of Paul and frighten her away again. Dammit, he swore silently, just when everything was going great with them.

"Look, there's a change girl," Andra said, cutting into Drew's thoughts. "Over there." She pointed to one of the farthest aisles, where a statuesque blonde in a scanty costume was busy making change from the coin dispenser strapped securely around her waist.

While Andra waved the girl over, Drew quickly

checked the aisles, making a mental note of the least crowded one in case they had to make a quick getaway. When he checked out the glass doors, he felt the skin on the back of his neck tighten. The other gorillalike man, shorter but meaner looking, was blocking the exit. Drew resolved to get Andra out of there immediately.

"Andra, we're running out of time. Why don't we . . ."

The sudden, deafening shower of coins—a rain of silver dollars—hitting against the metal container drowned him out.

"I hit it . . . I hit it!" the winner screamed hysterically, jumping up and down in front of the wildly flashing machine only eight or nine slots away from them. "I hit the jackpot!"

If the chubby young man had yelled "Fire," he could not have started a greater commotion. In a rush, people abandoned the slots they were playing, as well as nearby gambling pits, and came stampeding down the aisles.

As if that were just what he'd been waiting for, the big ape of a man started toward Drew, pushing his way easily through the crowd. By prearranged signal, the other man moved from the exit to join him.

Drew stepped in front of Andra automatically, shielding her with his body. "Andra, listen to me . . ."

"My God, look at that!" She laughed, craning her neck to see past his shoulder as the jackpot winner, tears rolling down his cheeks, was frantically filling up a large cardboard pail with silver dollars. "I've never believed these . . ."

"Andra!" Drew cut her off sharply. "Get over to the money cage—now!"

"What? But . . ."

"Don't argue." Grabbing her by the shoulders, he shook her. "Just go! Wait for me there." He turned her around, propelling her in the direction of the heavily guarded cage, but it was too late. The two men closed in on them, one on either side, blocking off the aisle.

"We wanna talk to you, Ramsey," said the man who'd been trailing them.

Andra froze as she recognized both men and realized that they weren't casino guards as she'd assumed.

"I'm busy right now," Drew said coolly. "Some other time."

"This won't take long," the other man said with a smirk.

"Okay, what do you want?"

The first ape jerked his head toward the exit. "Outside . . . in the car."

"Are you kidding?" Drew laughed harshly. "I'm not going anywhere."

"We just wanna talk," the second man said with a casual shrug. "Don't make no trouble, huh?"

Drew looked at Andra with concern. She was still in a state of shock, but she seemed all right otherwise. He turned his attention back to the two hoods. "Neither one of you looks very bright, but you can't be dumb enough to try anything in here . . ." He indicated the people still rushing down the aisles, crowding around the jackpot winner. A bomb could go off at that point, he knew, and nobody would pay any attention to it. He kept up his bluff. "Not with all these witnesses."

"Hey, who knows what could happen . . . even in here, huh, Frankie?" the first man said with a big, friendly smile.

"Anything could happen," agreed Frankie with a broad smirk. "A person could fall down, for instance, and get trampled in this crowd."

Andra gasped loudly. She was still unable to move and looked deathly pale. Her face mirrored the horror she'd felt when they'd visited Paul in the hospital.

"She belong to you?" Frankie asked, taking a step toward Andra. "Nice." His hard eyes moved over her body in a deliberately lewd manner. "Real nice. It'd be a shame if something was to happen to such a . . ."

"Okay, you win," Drew said with barely contained fury. "Just leave her out of it and I'll go with you."

"No!" Andra cried brokenly. She wanted to scream, to call attention to what was happening, but the look on both men's faces warned her of the consequences to Drew.

"I'll be all right, love," Drew said softly, reassuringly. "If these . . . gentlemen wanted to harm me, they'd have done it already. And they wouldn't leave you here as a witness."

A big grin split Frankie's ugly face. "Right."

"We just got a message for him, from a friend," his partner explained solicitously. "It's personal."

"Andra, wait for me over by the money cage," Drew said, enunciating each word clearly. He wanted to make sure that he was getting through to her in her dazed state. "I'll be right back." A mocking look passed between the two hoods, freezing Andra's blood. Flanking Drew, they started down the aisle toward the exit.

In a state of helpless terror, Andra remained frozen to the spot. Time slowed down until it was as drawn out as her heartbeat. She watched Drew walk away from her as if she were watching a movie in slow motion. The jackpot winner moved slowly toward her, a cardboard bucket filled with silver dollars in each arm, a retinue of brand-new friends at his heels. Just as he was about to pass her, Andra watched her hands glide up and knock both boxes out of his arms, sending silver dollars flying in all directions. And then the movie speeded up, became as frantic as a Keystone comedy.

With a strangled cry, the hapless winner threw himself flat out on the floor, flailing his arms and legs about in a vain effort to cover his dispersed treasure with his body. People were falling to their knees, crawling over the carpet, all over each other as they fought to scoop up as many silver dollars as they could.

Drew turned toward the commotion. Sizing up the situation instantly, he shoved his elbows into his captors' stomachs. They staggered back and, bumping into a couple scrambling out on all fours just behind their legs, toppled over them. Frankie screamed in pain as someone stepped on his fingers. His partner was clawing the carpet, trying to grab on to something to help him get back on his feet. Assuming that he was after her stash of silver dollars, a tiny but spunky old woman began beating him over the head with her pocketbook.

Andra and Drew just made it out of the aisle before a crew of casino guards and pit men went rushing into the melee in an attempt to bring order. Quickly overwhelmed by the crawling, yelling, shoving crowd, they went down in a tangle of arms and legs like Keystone cops.

9

~oooooooooo~

That was quick thinking on your part, love," said Drew as he pulled Andra into the empty elevator with him. Before the doors slid closed, he pressed the button to the twenty-third floor and laughed loudly. "But did you have to wreck the whole casino?"

"It's not funny," Andra protested, out of breath from the long run down the hallway that connected the casino to the hotel.

"Not funny? It was hysterical." Drew fell back against the metallic Art Deco interior as the elevator rushed upward without sound or discernible movement. "Didn't you see how those two apes went down like a sack of rotten potatoes?"

An instant replay of the scene unreeled in Andra's mind, making her laugh in spite of herself. "And that little old lady? Did you see the way she was beating the big guy on the head with her pocketbook?"

"Yes." Drew was laughing so hard, tears glistened in his eyes. "But the best . . . the best one was the guy who won the jackpot stretched out on the floor like a polar-bear rug, trying to cover his hoard of silver dollars."

Andra sobered instantly. "That poor man," she murmured guiltily, but the image of him flailing about on the floor in a greedy frenzy made her burst into hysterical giggles again. "Oh, I'm awful." She bit down on her bottom lip until she was able to suppress the laughter. "Do you think he'll get his money back?"

"I'm sure he will." Drew brushed the tears away from the corners of his eyes, which still gleamed wickedly. "The casino guards will see that he does," he assured her as the elevator doors parted soundlessly. Instantly on the alert, Drew put his arm out to hold Andra back. Sticking his head out of the doorway, he carefully scanned the hallway. When he was satisfied that it was deserted, he let her out but, holding tightly onto her hand, kept her close to his side. "That's if they can get themselves untangled," he added with a wry grin as he led her down the luxuriously carpeted hallway.

"Drew, where are we going?"

"Right here," he replied easily. He stopped in front of room 2303. He already had the key—one of a bunch dangling from his key chain—in his hand and quickly opened the door.

"But when did you get this—"

"Andra, I've got to call downstairs immediately," Drew cut her off bluntly, pushing her into the room without ceremony. After quickly scanning the hallway, he followed her inside, double locking the door behind him. "Do me a favor, love," he tossed over his shoulder as he made straight for the phone that rested on one of the end tables flanking the mauve velvet sofa. "I could use a drink. I'm sure you could too." His long fingers pointed out the commercial-size bar taking up the length of one wall before he quickly punched out a telephone number. "Would you mind?"

"Of course not." She certainly could use a drink. When Andra stood in front of the frosted glass shelves, which displayed bottles of every conceivable variety of liquor, she asked, "What do you want?"

"Brandy's fine," he said to her. Into the receiver he ordered tersely, "Ramsey here. Get me security. Fast."

As Andra poured out two brandies, she noticed that her hands were trembling. The rush of adrenaline that had propelled her through her actions in the casino and the long run down the hallway had dissipated. So had her mood in the elevator, which she realized now had been a hysterical reaction to what had happened. She suddenly felt drained.

On wobbly legs, she carried one of the snifters over to Drew, who waved his thanks with the cigarette he'd just lit while he carried on an intense conversation. Continuing on to the sofa, Andra sank down onto the plush velvet cushions. A couple of swallows of brandy steadied her hand while she took in the luxurious hotel suite.

The hotel room was a stunning blend of Art Deco furnishings. French marble and brass predominated. Huge panels of ormolu partitioned the living room from the bedroom; the ground gold metal gleamed richly under the light from the crystal fixtures. Glass—

etched, beveled, black, and mirrored—was everywhere, reflecting the bold, streamlined furniture, reflecting the room back on itself so that it appeared double, doubly luxurious.

Andra's attention, however, became fixed on two rather mundane objects: a suit of evening clothes identical to the one Drew was wearing that was still wrapped in protective plastic from the cleaners, and an open carton of Drew's brand of cigarettes lying on the white marble table in front of her.

Andra's hand was shaking again when she took another swallow of brandy.

"Sure, it's still on," she heard Drew say. Putting out his cigarette, he checked his watch while he listened intently to the voice on the other end of the line. "Okay, I'll wait for you to get back to me." He hung up.

Andra set her brandy glass down on the cocktail table next to the carton of cigarettes.

"I'm sorry, love," Drew said, stepping over to her, "but I had to give security a detailed description of those two . . . charming gentlemen. They tell me everything's still a mess down there." He laughed as though trying to recapture their earlier mood. "Even if those two manage to get away, they won't get back in without being spotted."

Sitting down next to Andra, Drew noticed that her hands were clenched tightly in her lap. "I'm sorry you had to get involved in that." He placed his free hand over hers reassuringly. "But it's really nothing to worry about."

Andra pulled her hands away and met Drew's eyes with a level stare. "Is this *your* hotel room?"

There was the slightest of pauses; then he nodded matter-of-factly.

"You mean last night, all the time you kept insisting that there wasn't a hotel room to be found in the whole city of Las Vegas, you knew you had this room?"

Drew took a careful sip of brandy. "That's right."

"You deliberately lied to me, made a fool of me?"

"Yes, I lied," he admitted simply and unashamedly. "But it wasn't because I wanted to make a fool of you." He stared down into the amber liquid he was swirling around in his glass. "I haven't been able to live at the house since you left. I couldn't have stayed there last night either, without you." He looked up at her then with dark, troubled eyes. "I just wanted you to be with me as much as possible. I knew that the only chance we'd have of working things out between us was if we stayed at the house together the way we had before."

"There's no chance of our working things out, not now," Andra said with more regret than anger. "I told you nothing has changed—except for the worse."

"That's not true," Drew insisted. "You've just got to give it a—"

"My God, Drew," she cut him off, "didn't you see what just happened? What might have happened if . . ." She was unable to continue, to put her worst fears into words.

"Andra, listen to me," he pleaded intensely as he moved closer to her. "I know you're scared right now. What happened was very scary, but that's exactly what it was meant to be." He put his hand lightly on her knee. The warmth of his touch had the same drugging effect on her as his voice. "Somebody, and I know who it is, is just trying to frighten me out of going to the game tonight. It's the oldest trick in the book." He took a long, hard pull on his drink and then set the glass down sharply on the cocktail table. "But he obviously doesn't know me very well."

"You're not going to the game?" Andra breathed incredulously, her eyes wide with fear. "Not after what just happened?"

"Andra, you've got to trust me," Drew insisted forcefully. "I know what I'm doing." With a hopeless sigh, she shook her head and turned away from him. "This is my world," he continued. "I know you hate it, but you don't really know anything about it." Taking her by the shoulders, Drew turned Andra around, forcing her to face him. "I know it like I know every card in the deck. Those two apes are right out of central casting. They're clichés, amateurs, penny-ante creeps."

Drew searched Andra's face to see if he was getting through to her. His fingers tightened around her shoulders when he realized that he wasn't. "Andra, real hit men wear business suits these days. You couldn't tell them from bankers. And they're pros. If *they* were out to get me, believe me, they would."

"Oh, that's very comforting," she cried. Pulling away from him, she jumped to her feet. "I feel so much better now!"

"Christ, Andra, do you think I'd ever involve you in a dangerous—" The sharp ring of the phone cut Drew off and made Andra jump. He slid all the way over to the end table and grabbed the receiver. "Yes?" With his back to her, he listened to what the other party had to say. "No problem," Drew answered, his voice sure and hard. "I'll take care of it. Be right down." He hung up and got slowly to his feet. "I have to go to the game."

Without a word, Andra walked over to the revolving cylinder that was crammed with the very latest in stereo and video equipment. She fought to harden herself against him. He wasn't going to smooth-talk her this time.

"I'm going to the game, Andra," Drew repeated softly. He held his hand out to her. "Aren't you coming with me?"

"No."

She'd barely breathed the word, but it had a finality that chilled Drew's blood. His hand dropped slowly to his side. "Will you be here when I get back?"

"No."

Drew was stunned by the intensity of the pain that shot through him. It felt as if someone had thrust a hand deep in his groin and ripped a piece out of him. He was unable to move, to take his eyes off Andra, even though it tore him up knowing that he might never see her again. She'd never looked more beautiful to him.

He was suddenly furious with her for doing this to him, for having the power to hurt him so deeply, but he'd never wanted her more. He wanted to pick her up and throw her down on the bed, to make love to her until she was as consumed as he was by the hunger that was eating him up just from looking at her.

Andra saw the pain twisting Drew's rugged face, felt the intensity of his desire clear across the room. Hope surged through her. If he loved her, if he'd really changed, then he couldn't choose a poker game over her this time. They might still be able to work things out between them.

Drew carefully released the breath that had broken off inside him, and it came out in pieces. He felt a muscle twitch uncontrollably in his jaw, and he knew that he was just an instant away from crawling to her, begging her to stay. She would only despise him more. Turning quickly, he started for the door.

As Andra watched Drew walk away from her for the second time that evening, she was gripped by the same helpless panic. She was vaguely surprised that she wasn't angry with him as she felt she should be. All she cared about was his safety. She didn't know how she could survive his being hurt.

The vicious faces of the two hoods flashed in her mind. What if they were still waiting for him downstairs? And she suddenly remembered the salesman's jeering threat to wipe Drew out. What might he do when Drew exposed him?

Drew hesitated before turning the doorknob, as if he were having second thoughts—or was he hoping that she was? Andra held her breath. Drew pulled the door open.

"No, don't go!" she heard herself cry, rushing over to him without having made a conscious decision to do so.

Drew turned when he heard Andra call out to him, so he was caught off balance when she threw herself into his arms without restraint. Falling back against the door, he slammed it shut with his back and his arms went around her in a fierce hug. "Thank God," he murmured hoarsely in her hair.

They clung to one another for an endless moment, shaking in each other's arms. Then Andra lifted her head from Drew's chest, his heartbeat still pounding in her ear. "Drew, please don't go to the game," she implored desperately.

"I've got to go, love. I've made a commitment to finish this job," he insisted ruefully. "I'm only doing it for us." His hand moved to smooth her hair off her face. "It'll be okay. Come with me, you'll see."

"No," she gasped, fear clouding her eyes again. "Please, I'll do anything you want . . . anything." Her arms went up to circle his neck, to hold him and keep him safe. "Drew, I'm begging you, stay with me . . ."

"Andra, I—"

". . . make love to me!" She felt every muscle in his body stiffen, but he didn't move, wouldn't—or couldn't—answer. She pressed her body closer to his. "I'm *begging* you," she repeated almost angrily. "Isn't that what you wanted?"

"No. *This* is what I wanted," he muttered thickly, his hand sliding into her hair, "you to love me again."

"But I do love you," she admitted miserably, "even though I'm not sure I want to. I've never stopped loving you."

A groan tore out of him that was crushed on her lips when his mouth came down on hers. Love and loss, joy and pain, a blind aching hunger were all in Drew's kiss. All were in Andra's response. No longer able to deny the love she felt, she gave herself up to him utterly, letting him take what he wanted, giving him more than he dared ask for.

"My God, do you know what you're doing to me?" he got out raggedly when he pulled his mouth away from hers. "I won't be able to concentrate on a single card for the rest of the night."

"Good." She laughed breathlessly and brushed his lips with hers. Her tongue flicked out to softly tease him.

"That's not fair," he rasped, but his tongue slid sensuously over hers, making her moan. "We've got to stop this." He buried his tongue inside her. Just for a moment, he told himself, she was so warm and delicious and he'd been denied for so long. But the more he tasted her, the more he wanted. The feel of her soft, yielding body straining against his was rapidly driving him up the wall, beyond control. He dragged his mouth away.

"If we don't stop this now," he warned thickly, "I won't be able to stop at all."

"Don't stop," she breathed, her eyes dazed with love and longing, her body melting utterly into his. Vaguely, Andra realized that she was giving herself much too completely, that she should hold back some small part of herself, if only in self-defense. What if Drew rejected her? But she could feel desire, like coils, tightening every muscle of his long, hard body, and she knew that he wanted her as much as she wanted him. With a ragged sigh, she kissed the tiny vein beating violently in his jaw. "Please don't stop."

His muttered curse brushed her temple before his lips did. "We've got to stop, love," he got out with difficulty. "The game."

Drew heard Andra's shocked intake of breath, felt her stiffen; then all feeling seemed to go out of her and her body went limp. Her arms slipped from around his neck and fell to her sides, a dead weight.

"Andra, the game won't take long," he was quick to assure her. "I've got the trap all set. Then afterward . . ." His hand slid down her back to press her hips tightly against his so she could feel for herself how much he wanted to make love to her. When he got no response, his other hand went up to tangle in her hair, tilting her face up to his. He searched her eyes intensely. The soft glow of love no longer lit them; they were dark with the pain of betrayal.

Guilt and anger twisted inside Drew. He'd sworn that he'd never be the cause of that look again. His fingers smoothed her fine, silky hair. "Andra, I'll make it up to you, I swear. Afterward, I . . ." He finished the sentence on her mouth, sealing his promise with a fierce kiss.

She didn't pull away from him as he'd feared. She let him kiss her, but her lips were cold and tense. He could feel her disappearing in his arms, and he knew that there wasn't going to be an afterward. The fear of losing her ripped through him. His mouth moved urgently on hers, desperately. Just as her lips were softening, warming again, she pressed tense hands against his sides and pushed away from him.

"You'd better go," she said. There was no anger in her tone, no emotion whatsoever. She'd simply given up on him. And why not, Drew thought in self-disgust, when he'd gone and ruined everything again.

Drew was only half right. Andra *had* given up, but it was on herself, on ever being able to reach him with her love. She was sure now that she'd never mean more to him than a poker game. She stepped back, giving him clear access to the door. When she spoke, her voice was flat and lifeless. "You'll be late for the game."

"Screw the game!" he bit out savagely. His hand reached out to grab her and haul her back into his arms. "I don't give a damn about the game." Strong arms tightened around her, crushing her to him as if he meant to make her part of him. "You're all I care about." His mouth took hers with a hunger that sought to consume, ripping through her numbness, shattering all her defenses.

With a muffled cry, her mouth opened to him, eager to be consumed, longing to consume, and she wrapped herself around him. A tremor shook his powerful body, shivering all through her; then his kiss gentled. With long, slow strokes of his tongue, he told her of his need for her until tears burned behind her eyes and she clung to him mindlessly.

Tears glistened on Andra's lashes when Drew finally lifted his mouth from hers. "Drew, did you mean it?" she asked breathlessly, almost afraid to let herself believe him. "You're not going to the game . . . promise?"

"I'm sick to death of games," he grated. Sweeping her up in his arms, he turned to carry her to the bed. Her head fell onto his shoulder, and she kissed the pulse beating violently in his throat. "No game is worth the risk of losing you," he murmured in her soft, fragrant hair. "I learned that the hard way."

Dragging kisses over her temple, her eyes, her wet lashes, Drew set Andra down in front of the king-size bed. "And that's all my life is without you, one long, empty game."

Andra's trembling lips parted, but she was unable to

speak because of the intensity of the emotions filling her. She was barely able to breathe.

She stopped breathing altogether as his hands moved hungrily over her body. "You're the only thing that's real to me," he went on, his voice raw, "that's ever been real in my life." His fingers lingered caressingly on the high, soft curve of her breast. "The only time I feel real is when I'm touching you."

Suddenly impatient fingers moved to her back, searching for the opening to her gown. Finding the concealed zipper, they quickly slid it open; then, hooking onto the ruffled edge of her neckline, they pulled the gown down and away from her body with one urgent motion.

Drew was rougher than he'd meant to be. He usually undressed her slowly, savoring every moment, but he was too hungry for her. "I'm dying to touch you," he mumbled apologetically. He tugged the delicate chiffon gown from under her feet and tossed it halfway across the room.

Longing to touch him also, Andra ran her fingertips over Drew's pleated shirt front. She managed to undo his string tie and was fumbling one of the onyx studs open when he brushed her hands away.

"I'm not through with you yet," he said darkly, sending an uncontrollable shiver through her. "I haven't even started." His burning gaze swept over the white silk and lace chemise she wore. He remembered the last time she'd worn it, the night they'd celebrated their third anniversary. The memory of that love-filled night made his hands shake as they moved down the front of her body, seeking the warm flesh beneath the perfumed silk.

Shivers went through Andra, wave after wave of them, and she had to grab onto him to steady herself. Drew sucked in his breath and his lips parted when he saw the budding tips of her breasts straining against the sheer lace. Swiftly, he bent his head to catch one of them between his teeth and draw it into the moist heat of his mouth. She cried out, her nails digging into him, as she felt the fierce tug of his lips and teeth on her, the ever-widening ripples of pleasure spreading through her.

He made a sound of pure male satisfaction when he felt her nipple swell with excitement between his lips, and his hands continued moving hungrily over her body. But he soon grew impatient with the filmy barriers of lace and silk. He ached for the texture of her skin under his hands, the taste of her in his mouth.

Andra's breathing quickened as Drew slid his hands under the chemise, over the flare of her hips and the soft curve of her belly, making heat flow under her skin.

"Your skin is softer than the silk," he whispered thickly, his fingers gliding up past her waist and over her tingling breasts, taking the chemise with them. "Like warm satin!" Quickly, he pulled the intimate garment up over her head, releasing it in midair as his hands rushed back to her breasts. It fluttered down to the carpet like a white silk and lace flag of surrender.

There was no way she could resist him or deny him any part of her. When he lowered his mouth avidly to her breast, she arched against it, burying her hands in his hair to pull him closer still.

Drew moaned deep in his throat when he tasted the unbelievable sweetness of her, the scent of her skin ravishing his senses, and he sought to fill his mouth with her. Instead of satisfying his hunger, it made him hungry for more. It became impossible for him to touch her as gently as he meant to. He dragged his mouth away before he lost all control. "It's been too long," he explained raggedly. "I'm too hungry for you." He released her abruptly.

Andra swayed and her eyes fluttered open, but they were dazed with sensation. Before she could focus on something other than him, Drew had lifted her off her feet and was sliding her into bed. She shivered as she felt cool satin against her heated skin.

Swiftly, Drew pulled her strappy sandals off and stripped the panty hose off her long, slender legs. He crushed the nylons in his shaking hand without realizing it, as his burning gaze moved over her body. Except for a tiny triangle of white lace, she lay naked. Her alabaster skin gleamed translucent against the satin sheet, and her ash-blonde hair was a luminous halo around her face. He wanted her so much he hurt.

Dropping the hose, Drew tore out of his dinner jacket. In his rush to undress, he pulled his pleated shirt off without bothering to undo the onyx studs, and they went flying in all directions. One of them bounced off the partition separating the bedroom from the living room.

Only then was Andra made aware of the ormolu panels shielding the bed. The unique metal had been burnished to a high gloss and was as reflective as a mirror—a "ground gold" mirror. Her mouth went dry and her pulse speeded up again as she stared transfixed at Drew's reflection while he quickly finished undressing.

With his tall, perfectly proportioned body, he looked like a statue of a golden god come to life. As Andra watched the gleaming play of muscles in his arms and chest, the corded strength of his legs, she ached to touch him all over, to feel him wrapped around her. She didn't know how she'd managed to live without him the past year, but she knew now why her life had been unbearably empty.

When Drew turned to face her, something tightened in Andra's throat, quivered deep inside her. She lifted her slender arms eagerly toward him, welcoming him into her embrace. A jolt of desire shot through him, and he knew that if he were to lie on top of her as he'd intended, he wouldn't be able to stop himself from taking her that instant. He had other plans.

Lowering himself slowly onto the bed, Drew slipped his head through the tender circle of Andra's arms but positioned his body so that he was lying on his side next to her. Her head arched back against the pillow, her lips parting in an irresistible invitation. He was about to kiss her when he noticed that her upper lip was slightly bruised.

"Look what I've done to your lip . . . my damn moustache," he muttered with regret. "I shouldn't have kissed you so hard, but—" with long, soothing strokes, his tongue glided over her swollen lip "—if you knew how much I've missed you, wanted you." He bit the corner of her mouth erotically, making her gasp. "And how often I've dreamt about this."

Compelled by the need to prove that he wasn't dreaming now—she was real, his for the taking—Drew moved impulsively. He wanted to lose himself in the liquid heat of her body, to feel her come apart in his arms, and recapture the shattering ecstasy he'd known only with her.

Inserting his muscular leg between her thighs, he parted them urgently and slid between them, burying his face between her soft, fragrant breasts. His ragged breath was hot on her skin, his voice raw with emotion. "Tell me you want me."

"Yes . . . I . . ." Andra's attempt to tell Drew how much she wanted him broke off on a moan when she felt his burning hands swallow up her breasts, pressing them together.

"Tell me!"

She tried, but all she could manage were small, incoherent sounds as his ravenous mouth kept moving from one aching tip of her breasts to the other as if he couldn't get enough of her. But her body told him unmistakably, as soft, sharp waves of pleasure vibrated through her.

"Yes!" he grated triumphantly when he felt her shaking beneath him. She reached for him blindly, barely able to breathe for wanting him, but he moved again.

His hands and mouth slid down her body, arousing her as only he ever had. The intense pleasure he found in touching and kissing her added to her excitement. Her nails raked his shoulders and she sought to pull him back up to her, but he eluded her again.

"This is what I couldn't forget—" he sank his teeth into her hip with barely controlled restraint "—what it's like making love to you." His flickering tongue soothed the tender spot and then traced the top edge of her panties as his hands slid under the elastic to find the rounded curves of her bottom. "I could feel you, taste you in my dreams."

Andra cried out as Drew's fingers dug into her flesh, bringing her hips up to meet his descending mouth. With a kind of adoration, he covered the lacy triangle with warm, wet kisses until she twisted wildly beneath him. Hooking the top of her panties, he peeled them off, lifting his mouth just enough to slide them past. When he lowered his mouth again, it was to claim her utterly.

Liquid fire flickered through her with every swirling caress of his tongue, flared intensely as his caresses quickened and deepened and she caught fire. She quivered, incandescent, and melted over him.

With one powerful motion, Drew surged up her body and buried himself in her. Andra's shudder echoed his when she felt the full extent of his possession, his hard male heat setting her on fire again, combining with her heat until they were fused together and it was all one burning convulsive explosion.

10

~oooooooooo~

Satin sliding against her bare skin, Andra stretched the length of her body as luxuriously as a cat. Still blurred with sleep, her eyes fluttered open reluctantly. It took a moment before she realized where she was. A languorous smile played on her lips when it occurred to her that, between this bed and the one at the hotel, she'd spent more time between the sheets in the past twenty-four hours than in the past year.

Through barely open lids, she caught a sliver of desert, its stark outline melting under the transforming glow of the setting sun. The fiery hues of the sunset streaking across the sky spilled over the balcony and through the picture window of the master bedroom, turning the pale yellow walls amber, the ivory satin sheets the color of warm flesh.

Andra closed her eyes, unwilling to let anything intrude on her delightful languor, to let go of the happiness that went as deep as her bones. Disconnected images of the day she'd just spent with Drew filled her mind like leftover fragments of a dream: the two of them laughing like kids as they put together a typical Vegas breakfast from the "45-course hot and cold gourmet buffet for only $1.95"; the wind whipping her face and hair, the excitement pounding in her veins as they raced on horseback over the winding trails; the lazy picnic in the clumpy shade of a Joshua tree while the horses dozed nearby; the long, sensuous shower, the water sliding between their bodies, the soapsuds growing warm under her hands as she slowly lathered his skin. . . .

Andra's hand slid searchingly over the sheet. Her eyes shot open when all she touched was cool satin. Quickly scanning the bedroom, she found Drew sitting in front of the large Oriental trunk in the far corner. He was fully dressed except for his dinner jacket, which hung from the back of the chair he'd carried there, and his shoes, which were underneath the chair.

He was using the wide, lacquered top of the antique trunk as a table—a poker table, obviously. He'd just finished dealing the last card in an imaginary game of five-card stud.

Andra pulled herself up against the headboard, automatically tucking the sheet around her naked body. Although Drew was sitting in profile and his concentration on the cards seemed total, he was immediately aware of her movement. He turned his head, and a warm smile softened the tense lines of his face. "How are you doing, sleepyhead?"

"Fine. I . . . you're up?"

"I didn't have the heart to wake you." He scooped

up the cards and got to his feet in the same easy motion. "You were sleeping so deeply."

"I can't imagine why."

"It must have been all that desert air and sun," Drew said teasingly as he came toward her.

"I'm sure that's the reason," she returned, her eyes glowing with the same love and wry humor as his.

"How are you feeling?" He sat down on the edge of the bed. "Any . . . repercussions?"

"Repercussions?"

"You said you hadn't gone horseback riding in a long time. Do you feel sore or achy?"

That wasn't the only thing she hadn't done in a long time. "A little sensitive in some areas, but . . ." She laughed throatily. "I don't think it's from horseback riding, although it certainly didn't help."

Drew laughed; it was warm and sexy and went right through her. Bending forward, he dropped a kiss on the tip of her nose. "You'll have to show me where it hurts"—softly, he brushed her swollen lips with his—"so I can kiss it and make it better."

"I think I've had all the kissing I can handle for one weekend," she murmured, somewhat amazed to find that she could still blush at her age.

"And I think you greatly underestimate your capacity." A wicked smile, which was also a promise, lit up his dark eyes as he straightened up.

Andra sighed a bit ruefully. "All I know is I can't seem to get through a weekend without ending up in bed with you."

Drew's smile faded, and when he spoke his tone was no longer playful but deep and intense. "I intend to do everything in my power to keep it that way."

It occurred to Andra—as it had several times that day—that Drew was assuming that everything had been settled between them and she was back to stay. Once again, feeling too caught up emotionally to be able to think clearly, she deliberately changed the subject. "I can't believe I slept so soundly that I didn't hear you get up or get dressed."

"That's because I was as quiet as a little mouse—and I got dressed in the guest room." He swung his long legs up onto the bed and, crossing them, sat there Indian fashion. As Andra watched with perplexed amusement, he began smoothing the satin sheet out in front of him. "Besides, I kept you up so late last night and dragged you out of bed so early this morning, you deserved to sleep." Effortlessly, he fanned the deck of cards out on the flattened sheet, face up. "And I thought I'd use the time to practice."

"Practice what?" Andra pulled her legs up to give Drew more room and, tucking the sheet around them, hugged them against her chest. "Card tricks?"

"Stacking the deck." He slid her a rakish smile. "See if you can catch me."

"Fat chance!" Andra laughed. "But I'll give it a try." Resting her chin on her raised knees, she peered intently down at the sheet. With deceptive ease, Drew's right hand skimmed over the cards while his left hand scooped up the entire deck.

Andra couldn't help admiring the way Drew's long, elegant fingers moved. But, as carefully as she watched him, she never saw him palm the three aces and drop them on top of the pack. "I thought we weren't going to work on the book today."

Drew finished shuffling four mediocre cards between each of the three aces and put an invisible crimp in the corner of the top card. "The book?" he murmured vaguely. He pushed out the bottom card of the "stock" he'd just built to make it protrude slightly from the deck when he slid it over to Andra. "If you'd be so kind as to cut."

Andra cut the cards at the "jog," exactly as Drew had set it up, but her action was automatic. She was staring at Drew's ruffled evening shirt as if she'd just noticed it. She suddenly realized why he was practicing stacking the deck—that was how he planned to trap the cardsharp. "You're going to the game tonight, aren't you?"

With one concealed move, Drew reversed Andra's cut, bringing the deck back to where it was before. "Of course."

"But last night you promised me you wouldn't go to the game," she said slowly, still unable to believe that he would deliberately lie to her about something so important. "You promised."

"And I kept my promise," he countered. Quickly and smoothly, he dealt five hands face up. "I didn't go to the game last night."

"But I didn't mean just last night."

"I did." He gave her a puzzled look. "And I thought you did too."

"How could you think that?" she cried, sitting back up against the pillows. "Why would I be any less afraid for you tonight than I was last night?"

"Because last night you were frightened by those two punks, which is understandable, but I explained the situation to you," said Drew while gathering up the cards with both hands and easily palming the aces.

"That was the whole purpose of their ploy, to keep me from going to the game. And thanks to you, it worked."

"It worked all right," Andra muttered under her breath. "It got you what you wanted too, didn't it?"

There was no reaction whatsoever from Drew, though Andra thought she saw a slight break in his rhythm as he continued shuffling the cards. She wasn't sure whether he hadn't heard what she'd said or whether he simply refused to deal with it.

Drew completed the false shuffle in silence, then slid the deck over to Andra; when he spoke, his voice was tight. "Cut."

Andra pulled the deck apart and slammed the top half down on the bed. "I thought you were sick to death of games."

"I am," he said evenly, meeting her eyes in a level stare, "but this isn't a game." Picking up both halves of the deck, he found that Andra hadn't cut to the jog this time. With the tip of his finger, Drew quickly found the crimped card and false-cut invisibly to it. "It's my job."

"Oh, well, that makes all the difference," she muttered sarcastically.

"It does to me." With quick, hard flicks of his wrist, Drew started dealing again. "I've never welched on a bet or a marker in my life, and I'm not about to start now."

Andra stared in amazement as Drew dealt her the exact same hand as before. He'd also dealt himself the identical cards again; the other three hands were different this time but just as unplayable.

"Andra, please try to understand," he went on,

making an obvious effort to remain calm and reasonable. "I've already accepted half of the fee up front, plus the more than fifty thousand dollars I won the other night." With a heavy sigh, he quickly gathered the cards. "I can't just walk out without finishing the job I started."

Andra sat up against her raised knees again. "Then give them back the money. What's fifty thousand dollars compared to your health or your life?" she pleaded, leaning toward him. "Drew, if it's money you're worried about, I have enough to get by on for a while. We'll work on the book together. I'll stay for as long as it takes to finish it."

"Very generous of you," he drawled with the strangest smile, cutting the cards together with hard, choppy movements. Even Andra could see how much his rhythm was off. "But what happens if I go to the game tonight?" An eight of hearts slid out of the deck, fell face down on the bed.

"Dammit!" he bit out savagely. "If just one card is out of order, the whole deal is wrecked!" Furiously, he threw the pack down on the bed, sending the cards flying, and turned on her. "What happens if I go to the game tonight, Andra? Will I find another note on the bed when I get back?"

Andra gasped. "That's not fair."

"And that's not an answer." His eyes held hers unflinchingly as he waited for her reply. Andra found that she couldn't let herself think about what would happen. It hurt too much. Drew saw the answer in her eyes. "That's what I thought."

"Drew, please don't go to the game."

He turned away from her and began collecting the

cards, which were strewn all over the sheet. "This is the last game of the weekend tournament. The last chance I'll have to catch the hustler." He had to stretch to reach the cards lying at the foot of the bed. "I understand he won very big last night, and if I don't—"

She cut him off sharply. "How do you know that?"

"Because I spoke to security on the phone this morning while you were getting dressed." When he saw the betrayed look in her eyes, he added, "Andra, I had to tell them why I didn't show up for the game."

"And did you tell them why?" She laughed harshly. "I'm sure the boys must have loved that!" Suddenly, she had to get away from him. She moved to get out of bed on the other side, but with his customary speed and dexterity, Drew dropped the cards and grabbed onto her arm, pulling her back.

"Yes, I told them why!" He tugged on her arm and she fell back against the pillows, the satin sheet sliding off her body. "My wife was so upset about what happened in the casino, I couldn't leave her because she means a helluva lot more to me than a damn poker game!"

In one powerful motion, Drew went up on his knees and pulled Andra up with him. He wrapped his arms around her, crushing her bare breasts against his chest, burying his face in her neck. "God, Andra, let's not argue about this any more," he pleaded. "We've had such a wonderful day, let's not spoil it." His breath was warm on her bare skin, his voice as compelling as the arms that held her tight. "I don't know about you, but it's been almost a year since I've been this glad to be alive."

Andra felt a rush of love go through her, the beginning of that loss of self she always experienced when he held her. She pressed trembling hands against his sides to push away from him so she could think clearly; her senses were already slipping out of her control. His muscles contracted at her touch, yet he let her go. But his dark eyes held her fast, as surely as his arms had.

"Weren't you happy with me today?" he asked softly, his fingers reaching out to smooth a stray lock of hair behind her ear.

"Yes, of course," she breathed, "but . . ." She never finished the sentence. Her mind was going too now, melting under the burning intensity of his gaze, the irresistible memory of shared love.

His fingers slid into her hair, drawing her face close to his. "Then the rest of it doesn't matter." Tenderly, he brushed his lips over hers. "This is all that matters, you and me." His mouth closed fiercely over hers and his powerful body surged against her with such force, she lost her balance and they sank down onto the bed.

Drew's kiss deepened as his body crushed hers into the satin sheets, but suddenly all Andra could feel was the cold, hard outline of the cards cutting into her back. They cut through the sensual and emotional daze she'd been lost in as well, bringing her back to reality. She dragged her mouth away and her hands, which had been clutching his shoulders, sought to hold him off.

"What is it?" he muttered thickly.

"The cards."

With a hoarse laugh, Drew sat up. "Sorry, love."

As Drew reached under her to get the cards out,

Andra slid over to the head of the bed and pulled herself up against the pillows. Her face and body were burning, yet she felt a chill shiver through her as she watched Drew reassemble the deck, the cards slipping effortlessly through his sure, quick fingers.

"That's exactly how I feel," she thought out loud, "just like those cards when you get your hands on them."

"Huh?" Drew smiled crookedly as though Andra had made a joke but he didn't get the punch line.

"That's how you play on my feelings. You . . . shuffle them around until you get the ones you want to come out . . ."

The smile died on Drew's face, and all the love and excitement he'd felt when he held Andra in his arms shriveled up inside him. He watched uncomprehendingly as she pulled the sheet up to her chin, hiding her body from him. He saw in her eyes that she'd already shut herself off from him emotionally.

". . . and I always end up exactly where you want me," she finished coldly.

"Andra, the only place I want you is with me," Drew objected, "in my life."

"In your bed, you mean!" she accused bitterly.

"I let that pass the first time, but I'll be damned if I'll let it pass again!" Ice-cold fury twisted inside Drew and his hand tightened around the pack of cards until his knuckles were as white as the sheet. "Are you saying that I deliberately manipulated you into bed? The way I remember it, *you* were the one who begged me to make love to you, and made it damned impossible for me not to!"

With one sure, agile motion, he swung himself off

the bed and stood towering over her. "I swore to myself that I wouldn't touch you unless I was sure of you, that I'd never let you do this to me again!"

Turning, he stormed over to the Oriental trunk as if he needed to put some distance between them in order to get himself under control. But when he looked back at her, his hand was still clenched tightly around the cards, and his rugged face was taut in the violet light of dusk that filtered through the picture window, spilling shadows everywhere.

"I've got you where I want you?" he went on sardonically. "That's a laugh. Half the time I don't know where the hell I stand with you."

"Drew, you know that I love you," Andra protested heatedly. He could accuse her of anything but that. "It's because I love you so much that I—"

"Prove it," he cut in bluntly.

"What?"

"Prove it! You demanded that I prove my love for you last night, and I did. I disregarded my commitments, everything I'd sworn to myself. You needed me, I was there." He tossed the pack of cards down on top of the antique trunk. "Well, I need you to be with me tonight at the game. I need to know that my wife loves me enough to stand by me even when I do something she doesn't approve of."

"It's not because I don't approve of you," Andra cried desperately, "but I can't . . . I won't stand by and let you do something that I know will hurt you!"

With a frustrated sigh, Drew sank down onto the chair. "I'm not going to bother to argue that point again because I know it won't do any good." Reaching under the chair, he slid his shoes out and began putting them on. "You agreed to meet me halfway, Andra, and you haven't. And the minute something goes wrong with us, you're ready to take off again."

Andra wanted to defend herself against Drew's bitter accusations, but she had to admit that he was right. Even now, she longed to run away rather than face an argument. It had always been that way, and she wondered whether it had something to do with her upbringing. Nobody argued with the Judge.

Wordlessly, she watched Drew finish tying his shoelaces. It was a miracle the laces didn't break off under the hard, angry tug of his fingers. She wished she could find a way to make him understand how she felt, but she couldn't think straight.

"The only way we're going to save our marriage," Drew resumed, getting to his feet brusquely, "is if we both try to work the problem out . . . fight it out, if we have to." He looked at her with dark, intense eyes. "You've got to stop running away and holding that over me as a threat!"

"I never meant to do that," Andra protested sincerely.

"But it's what you do." Tearing his dinner jacket off the back of the chair, he pulled it on with uncharacteristic carelessness. "Well, if that's the way it's going to be, you might as well leave me now. Let's just get it over with!"

Andra felt the blood drain from her face; every muscle in her body froze, paralyzing her.

Scooping the deck of cards off the top of the trunk, Drew started toward her. "I'm going on ahead," he said, his voice raw. He stopped beside the bed and dropped the cards in her lap. "It's your deal, Andra."

When she stared down at the cards uncomprehendingly, he added, "I'll send a car for you in an hour. You can use it to join me at the game, or you can have it take you to the airport."

She looked up at him with eyes that were wide with shock. Her lips trembled as they parted.

Drew held his breath as he waited for Andra to say something . . . anything! He felt as if he'd just bet his life on the turn of a card. And suddenly he knew that in a very real sense he had.

But she said nothing. He watched her fight to hold back the tears her pride refused to let her shed. Well, he had pride too. Turning, Drew walked abruptly to the door and pulled it open. "If you don't show up at the game, I'll stay at the hotel tonight," he tossed caustically over his shoulder. "I'm not coming back to an empty house and bed this time, so don't bother to leave a note!" He slammed the door behind him.

The brutal sound made Andra jump and shattered her defenses. Tears spilled down her face. She wiped them away impatiently. She couldn't afford the luxury of tears, there wasn't enough time. She had important things to think about—but she didn't even know where to begin.

The tears slid heedlessly down her face. One of them fell on top of the pack of cards lying in her lap. Her hand hesitated as she was about to brush the tear away, and she stared down at the cards for a long moment. Suddenly, she knew exactly what she had to do. It was the only thing she could do.

11

~oooooooooooo~

The last night of the weekend tournament always attracted a large crowd, but the word must have gone out that Drew was back in the game, because the majority of the spectators filling the Wild West saloon were massed behind the brass rail nearest him. The game had been going on for over an hour and still they came. Newcomers were quickly filled in on the events of the other night, so there was a constant buzz of excitement among the railbirds, an undercurrent of anticipation.

Drew was totally oblivious to everything going on around him. Before each deal, his eyes searched the crowd, looking for Andra. There couldn't have been more than eight or nine women present, so she would have been easy to spot even in that crowd. She wasn't there.

"Are you with us or with your public?" the loud, needling voice to his right demanded.

Drew brought his attention back to the smirking salesman who was busy adding a new tower to his rapidly growing fortress of chips. The big, black cigar clamped between his fleshy lips pointed upward victoriously. He'd just won the last pot with three backed-up aces.

Drew smiled coolly. He'd been waiting for over half an hour for those three aces, and it was his deal. Reaching over, he picked up several key cards from the discards lying in the center of the table. With a casual gesture, he used them to scoop up the aces, then dropped the lot on top of the pack.

Holding the pack snugly in his hand, Drew tapped it down on the baize several times as though he was evening it out. What he was really doing was testing the feel of the cards to make sure a "cooler" hadn't been switched into the game. It hadn't; the cards were still warm from handling.

Next, he ran his fingers lightly along the sides and both top and bottom edges of the deck without finding those almost imperceptible bulges that would have proven that the cards had been stripped.

Finally, with the pretext of separating the deck to get ready to shuffle, he gave it a quick riffle with his thumb. No dots or lines danced back and forth; the blue bicycle pattern on the back of the cards remained constant. He ruled out marked cards.

As Drew had anticipated, the sharp was too clever to attempt switching in another marked deck after what had happened the other night. He would be forced to mark the cards—and then, only key ones like aces, maybe kings—right there at the table, which meant that whatever he used to mark them with had to hidden on his person. That's what Drew was counting on.

A lifetime as a professional gambler had not only sharpened Drew's sense of touch but also his sense of smell beyond the normal range of the average person. He was able to detect the faint aroma of the special marking daub "shade workers" used—which was reminiscent of cleaning fluid—on the cards he was holding. He was ready to make his move.

Drew tossed a gray five-hundred-dollar chip into the center of the table. While the other four players were busy anteing up, he began stacking the deck.

Using a riffle shuffle, which allowed him to slow down the cards in his left hand while speeding them up in his right, he interwove three mediocre cards between the high ones he'd stashed on top of the deck. He then executed a couple of false chop shuffles without disturbing his stock. Putting a crimp in the card directly under the stacked ones, he set the deck down in front of the salesman for the cut.

"Boy, that was some pretty fancy shuffling," the salesman said with a malicious grin. He winked at the railbirds and ate up their laughing response as he cut the deck. "We country boys may not know how to shuffle fancy, but we sure know how to win."

"I'll bet you country boys know tricks we city slickers never dreamed of," Drew returned dryly.

The salesman let out a raucous laugh and his beady eyes gleamed, hard and sly. He'd made the cut just below the jog, but Drew easily found the crimped card and quickly reversed the cut, bringing the deck back to its original position.

Setting himself for the deal, Drew announced, "Five-card stud." The salesman clamped down on his cigar, and an expectant hush came over the crowd.

Swiftly, Drew dealt everyone the first card face down, then another one face up. He made a show of glancing at his hole card, although he already knew what it was, then deliberately covered it with his arm. His real interest was the other players' reactions to their cards.

With a fatalistic shrug, the urban cowboy threw in; with even less display of emotion, so did the white-haired executive. The compulsive gambler continued to peer at his hole card with bloodshot eyes as if he refused to accept the obvious.

Drew had stacked the deck with an unplayable assortment of deuces, fours, and sevens, and not even the wildest chance of making a flush or a straight, to force all three of them out of the game. For his trap to work, and for the rest of the cards to fall exactly as he'd planned, all three men had to drop out.

Tapping his nicotine-stained fingers nervously on the green baize, the compulsive gambler gave his cards one last defeated look. Reaching for his Scotch on the rocks, he folded.

"Looks like it's just you and me," the salesman shot challengingly at Drew.

Drew gave a bored shrug. "Looks like it."

A confident grin split the salesman's beefy face as he studied the cards. Drew had dealt him an ace in the hole with a queen showing; he'd also dealt himself an ace in the hole but was showing a jack. The salesman lifted ten black one hundreds off a stack of chips and dropped them into the pot. "One thousand," he announced loudly.

Drew merely called the bet and dealt the next card: a jack for his opponent, a seven for himself. The salesman could hardly wait to raise. Drew merely called again—he wanted to give the impression that he was staying, not betting his hole card.

Drew took a leisurely sip of his Perrier before dealing another jack to the salesman, an ace to himself. A restless murmur went up from the spectators, and they pressed against the brass rail. On the board, the cards now showed a pair of jacks and a queen for the salesman and an ace, a jack, and a seven for Drew.

The diamond ring flashed on his stubby hand when the salesman separated a tower of black chips from his fortress and pushed it into the center. "Five thousand."

Without a second's hesitation, Drew pushed two black towers into the pot. "See your five . . . raise you five."

The salesman blinked. He tried to get a look at Drew's hole card to see if it was marked, but Drew's arm was still resting casually over it, frustrating his attempt. He clamped his teeth down on his cigar with such force Drew half expected it to break off.

Coolly, Drew dealt the last up card: a nine for his opponent, making his hand a pair of jacks, a queen, and a nine; and a jack for himself, adding up to a pair of jacks, an ace, and a seven.

A low drawn-out murmur came from the railbirds as

they craned forward, then a strange silence, like a communal holding of breath. The salesman sipped his bourbon thoughtfully, and he took a full minute to consider Drew's cards, his eyes sullen.

Drew knew exactly what he was thinking. The best possible hand Drew could make, with his hole card, was a pair of aces or sevens to back up his jacks. Since he'd deliberately dealt two sevens to the dropouts, the salesman's only worry was whether Drew had an ace in the hole. If he didn't, then the salesman would take the pot because his ace in the hole matched the ace Drew was showing, and their pair of jacks canceled each other out, leaving the salesman's queen to beat Drew's seven.

Drew let him squirm for another minute while he pretended to weigh his next move carefully. Then slowly, almost casually, he put his hand behind a stack of gray five hundreds and slid twenty thousand dollars' worth of chips into the pot.

The salesman grinned around his cigar. He was sure that Drew was bluffing. Quickly he reached for his chips as Drew raised his arm, letting the salesman finally see his hole card. The salesman's mouth went slack, and tiny beads of sweat popped out on his upper lip. He pulled his hand back and folded his cards.

A communal gasp of surprise went up from the railbirds. Drew smiled. As he'd anticipated, the sharp had read his marked card for an ace and knew that Drew had the winning hand.

"Don't touch those cards," said Drew bluntly to the urban cowboy, who was about to reach over to collect them for his deal. "I'll explain in a minute." Pushing his chair back, he got to his feet.

Pete, the head cashier, who'd been watching for the prearranged signal, dashed out of the cage; the plainclothes guard pushed away from the bar. Together, they made their way over to the table.

"What's goin' on?" the salesman demanded. "Every night this guy's gotta pull something new." In his outrage, he forgot his country-boy accent.

"Someone's been hustling this game," said Drew grimly, fixing him with a stare. "And now I know who it is."

The salesman threw his head back with one of his raucous laughs, but it sounded forced. "Why, you're the one with the fancy shuffle, boy. We're all a bunch of amateurs compared to you."

"What seems to be the trouble, Mr. R.?" Pete asked as he stopped beside Drew. The plainclothes guard remained in front of the opening in the rail, blocking it with his massive body.

Drew pushed all the cards to one side of the table except for the three aces, which he turned face down on the baize. "These cards have been marked."

With looks of varying degrees of amazement, all the players, including the cardsharp, bent over to peer at the blue-backed cards. Murmuring excitedly, even the railbirds strained forward.

"Where are they marked?" asked the sharp contemptuously. "I don't see any marks, do you?" The other players whom he'd been addressing nodded their heads in agreement.

"It's very difficult to detect," Drew allowed dryly.

"Only an experienced shade man could have done such an expert job. But if you look carefully"— bending over, he pointed to each of the four corners of one of the cards—"you can see a faint, smoky glow."

Now that he'd pointed it out, the others were also able to see it. "I checked this deck out myself when we first started playing," he went on, "and it was clean. It had to have been marked right here at the table." He straightened up. "And whoever marked it still has the evidence on him."

"Well, gentlemen, there's a very simple solution to our problem," the head cashier suggested politely. "If you would all agree to be searched, we . . ."

"Nobody's going to search me," the hustler bellowed, jumping to his feet. His face darkened, and veins popped out on his thick neck. "Haven't you people ever heard of the fifth amendment?"

"I think you've got your numbers wrong," Drew corrected wryly. His left hand shot out to grab the sharp's wrist, and before the man realized what was happening, Drew had slid his right index finger over the large diamond ring the sharp wore. Releasing his wrist, Drew bent over and made an X on the back of one of the aces. When he picked up the card and held it up to the light, the smoky glow in the shape of an X was undeniable.

An "ahhh" of amazement went up from the crowd, as though they'd just witnessed a magician's feat of magic. Drew threw the card down on the baize. "I'm sure you'll find a jar of glow daub concealed somewhere on his person."

A growl of rage tore from the hustler's throat, twisting his thick features, and he took a threatening

step toward Drew. The cashier quickly moved between them. The sheer incongruity of a thin, five-feet
five-inch man trying to come between two powerfully
built men who were both well over six feet tall stopped
the hustler in his tracks.

"That really won't do, Mr. B.," Pete chided in his
thin, Sunday-schoolteacher's voice. "Not if you wish
to walk out of here without assistance." He shook his
balding head tolerantly; he might have been dealing
with a naughty schoolboy. "And I think I should warn
you that we won't forget you . . . or your two friends
from last night. We have . . . friends too."

The smile that stretched his thin lips was all the more
ominous for being so polite. "And if they should find
out that you were foolish enough ever to set foot in
Vegas again, or that you or your two friends should
inconvenience Mr. R. here, as you did last night,
well . . ." He paused with a heavy sigh as if he
couldn't bear even to think of what would happen.

The cardsharp's normally ruddy complexion turned
ash gray.

A smile of immense relief suffused Pete's lean face.
"I'm so glad we understand one another. Now, if you
don't mind, I think you'd better go with my friend
there." With a wave of his slender hand, he indicated
the plainclothes guard waiting by the rail. "There's a
small matter of returning the money you cheated
these gentlemen out of." A gentle push propelled the
stunned hustler in the direction of the guard. "I'm sure
you understand."

As Drew watched with ironic detachment, Pete
turned to the other players. His smile was purely
official. "All bets are off, gentlemen. You may cash in

your chips and any monies that we recover will be returned to you. I hope you'll allow us to pick up the tab on any expenses you may have incurred during your stay at The Xanadu. And please visit us again the next time you're in Vegas.

"After you, Mr. R.," Pete offered with a wave of his hand. Drew moved ahead of him through the opening in the rail. The excitement over, the players at the other tables resumed their poker games and the crowd began dispersing.

"That was better than the floor show, Pete," Drew said with a chuckle, reaching into his pocket for a cigarette.

"It couldn't touch your performance, Mr. R.," Pete returned with genuine admiration. "We're very grateful to you."

"Just doing my job. Cigarette?" He extended his gold cigarette case.

"No, thank you. I had to give them up," he explained ruefully. "High blood pressure."

"I can see why," Drew murmured, shutting the case on Andra's inscription. "But I didn't realize that The Xanadu had . . . friends."

"We don't actually," Pete admitted. "But these people just aren't afraid of the police. Threatening them with the mob always works."

"Thanks for taking care of it," said Drew when he finished lighting his cigarette.

"I'll get the remainder of your fee," Pete began.

"There's no rush," Drew muttered absently as he scanned the faces of the women in the dispersing crowd with troubled eyes.

"Is everything all right, Mr. R. ?" Pete asked solicitously.

"Sure." Drew forced a smile. "Thanks again, Pete. I'll see you tomorrow."

Drew scanned the crowd one last time before pushing through the swinging doors into the main gambling area of the casino. The flashing slots, the spinning roulette wheels, the raucous shouts from the dice pit, and the excitement-hungry crowd somehow added to his depression. He decided to have a quiet drink in the lounge, where a better-than-average jazz quartet was performing.

On his way to the lounge, Drew passed the wall-to-wall pay phones lining the hallway. A half dozen or so losers were busy making the same call: a desperate attempt to raise money. In spite of himself, he stopped and called the house. He let the phone ring a long time. There was no answer. On the off chance that he'd dialed incorrectly, he punched the number in again. Again, no one answered.

When Drew hung up, he didn't feel like stopping for a drink anymore. He decided to go up to his room instead. At least there he could drink himself blind if he felt like it.

As he let himself into his room, he was wondering whether Andra's flight to New York had already taken off or whether she might still be at the airport. His thoughts were sidetracked by the sudden realization that all the lights were on and music was pouring from the stereo. He came to a sudden halt when he recognized the melody. It had been almost a year since he'd played that record.

Drew quickly scanned the living room, but it was empty. Obviously the maid had left the lights on again. She probably listened to music while she worked, he reasoned, and had simply forgotten to turn it off afterward.

Undoing his string tie and the button in his collar, Drew started toward the revolving cylinder that housed the state-of-the-art stereo and video equipment. Tonight of all nights, he could do without that song.

His feet sinking into the thick carpet, Drew continued past the ormolu partition between the bedroom and the living room. He came to a dead halt again. It seemed to him that his heart literally stopped. Andra was sitting up on the bed.

She was so still that for an instant Drew wasn't sure whether she was real or a projection of his desires. The reflection of the lights bouncing off the ormolu panels bathed her in a golden glow, turning her ash-blonde hair into an incandescent halo and making her bare shoulders gleam. The yellow satin strapless evening gown she wore appeared molten, a river of gold flowing over every curve of her lovely body.

When Drew's heart resumed beating—in double time to make up for the lost beats—he noticed that Andra's attention was fixed on the cards that were lined up in front of her on the bedspread. She was playing solitaire, but was staring down at the cards with the intensity of a medium trying to divine the future. A bottle of champagne nestled in a silver ice bucket on top of the cart that was set within easy reach of the bed.

Shaking her head disgustedly at the cards, which refused to come out as she wanted, Andra turned to pick up her glass of champagne from the cart and saw Drew. Her breath caught and her hand hesitated for the fraction of a second. Hoping that Drew hadn't noticed, she sent him a dazzling smile and lifted her glass playfully. "Hi."

"Uh . . . hi," Drew stammered. He was thrown even more by her attitude than by her being there. That was exactly how Andra had planned it. She smiled inwardly when she saw him fumble his cigarette case and lighter out of his pocket while he walked slowly toward the bed. "I thought you'd left."

"No," she replied cheerfully, taking a sip of champagne. "I'm still here."

"So I see." He tapped the tip of his cigarette on the case with that staccato rhythm he used when he checked at poker—a sure sign of uncertainty. That knowledge had a more intoxicating effect on Andra than the champagne. He stared at her intently for a moment. "Then why didn't you come to the game?"

"I needed the time to think . . . about us." Putting her fluted glass down, Andra began gathering up the cards. "And to decide what I'm going to do next."

Drew finished lighting his cigarette and took a long, hard drag as if it were his last before facing a firing squad. "And?" He exhaled unevenly. "Did you decide?"

"Yes." Sliding over to the edge of the bed, Andra got to her feet. "I've decided to take your advice. I'm not going to run away this time. I'm going to stay and fight it out." Mischief sparkled in the depths of her expressive gray eyes as they met his. "On your territory, and with your weapons." She smiled. "Champagne?"

"Uh, yeah," Drew muttered distractedly, "but what do you mean, *my* weapons?"

"We've been going about this problem the wrong way, Drew," said Andra, sliding the bottle of Dom Pérignon '78 out of the ice bucket. "I think we should deal with it as if it were a poker game," she went on lightly while she poured him a glass of champagne and refilled hers. "Obviously, we each feel that we have an unshakable argument—or, in poker terms, an unbeatable hand. So let's both put our cards on the table. Whoever has the stronger hand wins. And the decision is final."

"Sounds interesting," Drew murmured, clearly intrigued.

Andra had counted on his being unable to resist a challenge. "Then you agree?" She offered him the glass of champagne.

He accepted it with a wry grin. "I'm game."

They clicked glasses, and the ringing, high-pitched sound the struck crystal made grated on Andra's nerves. She was far more worried about the outcome of this "game" than she'd realized. But she was determined to play it out to the end.

Taking a deep breath, she plunged ahead. "Earlier you said that it was my deal, so I'll put my cards on the table first. Then we'll see if you can top them." Her throat went dry. She took what she hoped looked like a casual sip of champagne.

The icy, bubbly wine soothed her parched throat while she mentally reviewed her "hand." When Andra looked up at Drew again, her gaze was sure and steady. "I love you very much, Drew. I want to be your wife again. I want to have your children." She spoke softly and slowly, pausing after each sentence like a dealer calling out the value of each card as it was dealt face up on the baize. "Drew, I know I can make you happy. We could have a wonderful life together . . . a *real* life with a home and a family and—" Her voice broke off as the importance of what she was "playing" for became too real for her.

Drew laughed warmly and with obvious relief. "It's no game, love. We're both holding the same cards." He took a step toward her. "That's exactly what I want too."

Andra stepped back. "There's just one catch, Drew. We can have all that only if you give up gambling for good. As a profession," she amended, "but that includes your job as a gambling investigator."

Drew took a long pull on his cigarette and then finished his glass of champagne while he studied her in that way he had when he was trying to determine whether an opponent was bluffing.

"Drew, you've got to make a clean break," Andra insisted. "It won't work otherwise, don't you see that?"

"Andra, I thought I'd already explained this to you," he said patiently as he set his empty glass down on the cart. "I want to get out of gambling . . . I'm trying. This job is the first step."

"Is that your best card?" She smiled incredulously. She'd obviously expected better from him. "It's not nearly good enough, compared to what I'm offering you."

"Well, it's the best I can do right now!" Drew took his frustration out on the cigarette as he squashed what was left of it in the ashtray. "Gambling is the only thing I know, Andra. It's the only thing I'm any good at."

Andra set her glass carefully down on the cart. "You're bluffing, Drew," she said evenly. She was shaking inside, but she didn't flinch under the furious look he shot her. "Not me—yourself."

Drew started to walk away from her, but Andra stepped quickly in front of him. Since he was hemmed in on either side by the cart and the bed, there was nowhere else he could go; he was forced to deal with her.

"You don't really believe that you couldn't find another job, do you?" she went on. "With your talent and intelligence"—she laughed suddenly, and her hand went up to muss his hair playfully—"and with that computer brain of yours?"

"Come on, Andra," Drew muttered tightly, twisting his head away. The motion was meant to make her think that he was trying to shake her hand off; in reality, he was trying to keep her from seeing the doubt and insecurity her words had brought to the surface. He was sure that would make her despise him.

"Drew, don't you realize," Andra persisted, "that the same qualities that have made you such a brilliant card player will make you a success at anything you want to be?" She had to tilt her face all the way to one side so she could look up into his. Drew was stunned by the love and admiration shining in her eyes. "Take the chance." An ironic smile tugged at the corners of her mouth. "You're a gambler. Gamble on yourself for a change."

It occurred to Drew that he was being rapidly outmaneuvered. Total silence hung between them; even the music had stopped. But Andra had programmed the stereo to replay the record, and in a moment the music started up again. The sensuous strains of the melody, the memories it evoked, made it even more difficult for Drew to think objectively. "Andra, I don't know," he muttered evasively, "I . . ."

"The choice is yours, Drew," Andra murmured, moving into his arms, giving him no choice at all. Her breasts brushed against him as she went up on her toes to nuzzle his ear. "Gambling . . . or me."

Drew's head jerked back. It was impossible to think at all with her warm breath tickling his ear, the feel of her pulling at his senses. He managed a sardonic smile. "Are you giving me an ultimatum?"

She laughed throatily, making his blood jump. "Just think of it as the showdown in poker." Her hands moved to twine in his hair and coax his face back to hers. "I've made my move." She nibbled playfully on his bottom lip. "Now it's your move."

Drew's fingers circled Andra's waist to hold her off, but they dug into her instead when she tugged at the corner of his moustache with her teeth. "You're not playing fair," he muttered thickly.

"No," she agreed, "I'm playing to win." Her tongue slid between his parted lips to tangle sensuously with his—a gambit she'd learned only too well from him. Drew groaned and his hands tightened around her.

Andra suddenly realized that she was playing a dangerous game. It would be so easy for her to lose herself in the feel of his body, the sweet, moist warmth of his mouth. Drew sought to deepen the kiss and take control of it. Andra threw her head back, barely escaping him.

"It's your move," she insisted, her voice shakier than she would have liked. "I've already put all my cards on the table."

Drew's hands moved over the soft, inviting curves of Andra's body. "A stacked deck if ever I saw one," he drawled wryly. The satin fabric of her gown felt as smooth as her skin under his hands but lacked her skin's warmth.

Andra could feel her body melting under Drew's sensual touch. She stepped back out of his reach before her mind dissolved as well.

"All right, Drew, I'll make it easy for you," she said, trying to keep her tone as firm as her purpose. "I've already told you what I want. I'll play you for it."

"What?"

"One hand of poker. If you lose, then you have to give up gambling as a profession for good. If I lose, you don't have to, and I promise to accept that and never complain about it again."

Drew laughed as though Andra had made a joke. It was only when she didn't laugh with him that he finally noticed the fierce determination in her eyes. "Are you serious?"

"Very." Stepping over to the bed, Andra reached down and picked up the deck of cards she'd left there before. "I told you I was going to fight with your weapons."

He stared at her incredulously for a moment. "Let me get this straight. You want to play a hand of poker—with me?" Andra nodded resolutely. "I thought you said you couldn't win with me."

"I'm willing to take my chances," she replied coolly. She held her hand out to him. "Is it a deal?"

Drew's innate sense of honor made him hesitate. It would be like taking candy from a baby. But it was her idea, and if it would finally settle this problem between them . . .

With an overconfident grin, which he tried to suppress but couldn't, Drew took Andra's hand. "It's a deal." Her handshake was firm—and very professional, he couldn't help thinking.

"We can play right here," Andra said as Drew scanned the living room searching for an appropriate place to play. "Right here . . . on the bed."

When Drew turned back to Andra, she was already sitting up on the bed. Sensing a ploy, he was about to protest her choice, but the look she was giving him was utterly guileless. She was obviously unaware of how seductive she looked.

As though she could barely wait to get on with the game, Andra patted a place for him on the bed beside her. Drew sank down onto the king-size bed but chose a safer spot, one directly across from her. Safer, up to a point, he realized once he'd settled in. The exquisite view her décolletage afforded would have put any man off his game.

"All right now," Andra began.

"Wait a minute, love," Drew said, suddenly remembering, "we can't play without chips."

"We can substitute something for chips," she said

with that patronizing tone a professional uses when forced to deal with a rank amateur. "People do it all the time."

Drew chose to disregard her condescension toward him—over what he was a master at!—even though it irritated the hell . . . was she trying to psych him out? Impossible, he assured himself quickly; she couldn't have played poker more than five times in her life. But she had watched him play any number of times.

"Drew, if you're not going to take this seriously," Andra protested, "then we may as well forget about it."

"No, uh . . . I was just trying to figure out what we can use instead of chips." With growing frustration, Drew dug into his pants pocket. "I don't usually have much change."

"And I don't have any." Andra indicated her strapless evening gown with a hopelessly forlorn gesture, intimating that, outside of that mere scrap of satin that clung, gleaming, to every curve of her body, she was utterly bereft of worldly possessions. She brightened suddenly. "I know—we can use kisses."

"Kisses?" he bit out between clenched teeth. *"Kisses!"*

"I don't have anything else," she said ever so innocently.

Drew caught a flash of pure mischief behind Andra's wide-eyed "innocent" look. So *that* was going to be her strategy. Well, two could play that game. He smiled. "Kisses it is."

"Oh, good." Picking up the deck, Andra began shuffling with considerably more skill than Drew would have given her credit for. "Let's see . . . what shall we play?'' she murmured, as excited as a little girl. "I know. Let's play draw poker with . . . something wild.''

"Andra!'' Drew gasped, always the purist.

"We've got to make something wild, Drew. It's no fun otherwise.''

Drew took a long, deep, steadying breath. His father had warned him against playing poker with women. But what a woman! She *was* trying to psych him out, and doing a damn good job of it. He forced an indulgent shrug. "Okay. One-eyed jacks?''

She frowned, clearly disappointed with so obvious a choice. "Let's make it the jack of hearts.'' Mischief sparkled in her silvery eyes again. "Hearts are wild.'' She was about to give the cards another brisk, efficient shuffle, but after pausing thoughtfully, she set the deck in front of him instead. "I think you should deal.''

"Me?'' Now Drew was completely thrown. Didn't she realize that she was literally putting her life in his hands? "You trust me to deal when you know I can make the cards do anything I want?''

"It's your choice, Drew,'' she stated simply. "It's got to be your deal.''

In a lifetime of gambling, Drew had known very few men who would have had the guts to make such an offer and with such cold-blooded nerve. If he wasn't crazy about her already, he would have fallen in love with her on the spot. As it was, he had to stop himself from grabbing her and throwing her down on the bed and . . .

"Well?'' she demanded.

Drew reached over and picked up the deck of cards. "You seem pretty sure of yourself.''

"Not really," Andra admitted, tilting her chin up proudly. "But I'll tell you what I'm betting on. I'm betting that you love me as much as I love you, and that you really want the kind of life I can give you." An irrepressible smile played on her soft lips. "You wouldn't have conned me into coming back to Vegas if you didn't."

Drew groaned inwardly. Talk about psyching out your opponent! He had to force himself to concentrate on his strategy while he reshuffled, the cards flying automatically through his expert fingers.

When he set the deck down before Andra, he was sure that he saw her hand tremble slightly as she made the cut. Yet she seemed very much in control when she leaned over suddenly and kissed him full on the mouth.

"Just putting up the ante," she explained, keeping her lips within easy reach. She had him so rattled, Drew was unable to react. "Aren't you going to put up your ante?"

Drew stifled a curse. He lowered his mouth to Andra's, trying to concentrate on duplicating the exact pressure and length of her kiss, to match the ante, without actually feeling and tasting her. It didn't work.

When he pulled back, the warm sweetness of her lingered on his lips, the fragrance of her skin continued to swirl around his senses. He cleared his throat. "Jacks or better to open," he reminded her gruffly while he quickly dealt them both five cards, face down.

Andra picked up her cards and eagerly arranged them. When she got a good look at them, she rearranged them. That obviously didn't make them any better. She sighed. "I pass."

"I'll open," Drew muttered, poker-faced, "with . . . one kiss." Bending over, he quickly brushed Andra's lips with his.

"I'll see your kiss," she returned seriously, brushing his lips as lightly with hers. "And I'll raise you a kiss." This time, her mouth closed over his. Slowly, she molded their lips together, moving with a sensuous tenderness that made his breath shorten and threatened his control.

Drew started to pull away, but using a favorite gambit of his, Andra nipped his bottom lip with her teeth, drawing it into her mouth where her tongue slid over it erotically. A shudder went through him. It struck Drew that she was beating him at his own game.

With a purely reflex action, born of his almost compulsive need to win, Drew grabbed Andra and pulled her against him. Her startled cry was muffled by the hard crush of his mouth, and she stiffened in his arms. But as his mouth moved with growing hunger over hers, he felt all resistance go out of her, and she melted, soft and warm, against him.

The cards fell out of her hand as she threw her arms heedlessly around his neck, her mouth opening to allow the deep, possessive thrust of his tongue, and Drew knew that he was lost.

He felt a surge of intense love and desire for her, an infinite tenderness that went as deep as his blood. She was utterly incapable of playing games, he realized. And whenever he felt her go all open to him like this, so was he.

"Okay," he grated when he dragged his mouth away from hers. "You win."

She laughed breathlessly and with a kind of surprise. "But you didn't see my cards."

With one powerful motion, Drew swept all the cards off the bed. "Take my word for it," he murmured thickly, lowering his mouth to hers again. "You've got an unbeatable hand."

Tears misted Andra's eyes, making the love that was reflected in them glow even brighter.

It occurred to Drew, as he pulled Andra down onto the bed with him, that sometimes you have to lose to win.

Silhouette Desire Romances

TAKE 4
THRILLING SILHOUETTE
DESIRE ROMANCES
ABSOLUTELY FREE

Experience all the excitement, passion and pure joy of love. Discover fascinating stories brought to you by Silhouette's top selling authors. At last an opportunity for you to become a regular reader of Silhouette Desire. You can enjoy 6 superb new titles every month from Silhouette Reader Service, with a whole range of special benefits, a free monthly Newsletter packed with recipes, competitions and exclusive book offers. Plus information on the top Silhouette authors, a monthly guide to the stars and extra bargain offers.

An Introductory FREE GIFT for YOU.
Turn over the page for details.

As a special introduction we will send you FOUR specially selected Silhouette Desire romances — yours to keep FREE — when you complete and return this coupon to us.

At the same time, because we believe that you will be so thrilled with these novels, we will reserve a subscription to Silhouette Reader Service for you. Every month you will receive 6 of the very latest novels by leading romantic fiction authors, delivered direct to your door.

Postage and packing is always completely free. There is no obligation or commitment — you can cancel your subscription at any time.

It's so easy. Send no money now. Simply fill in and post the coupon today to:-

**SILHOUETTE READER SERVICE, FREEPOST,
P.O. Box 236 Croydon, SURREY CR9 9EL**

Please note: READERS IN SOUTH AFRICA to write to:-
Silhouette, Postbag X3010 Randburg 2125 S. Africa

FREE BOOKS CERTIFICATE

**To: Silhouette Reader Service, FREEPOST, PO Box 236,
Croydon, Surrey CR9 9EL**

Please send me, Free and without obligation, four specially selected Silhouette Desire Romances and reserve a Reader Service Subscription for me. If I decide to subscribe, I shall, from the beginning of the month following my free parcel of books, receive six books each month for £5.94, post and packing free. If I decide not to subscribe I shall write to you within 10 days. The free books are mine to keep in any case. I understand that I may cancel my subscription at any time simply by writing to you. I am over 18 years of age.
Please write in BLOCK CAPITALS.

Name _____

Address _____

_____

_____ Postcode _____

SEND NO MONEY — TAKE NO RISKS
*Remember postcodes speed delivery. Offer applies in U.K. only
and is not valid to present subscribers. Silhouette reserve the right
to exercise discretion in granting membership. If price changes
are necessary you will be notified.
Offer limited to one per household. Offer expires April 30th, 1986.*

EP18SD